Trouble At Webster's

Long after the cabin was in darkness, Emily lay wide awake in her bunk. From the restless shifting and squirming above her, she knew that Libby couldn't sleep either. Emily wanted very much to talk to Libby, but she was afraid Pam might wake up and hear them. It was apparent that Pam didn't want anybody to know what the "bad news" was, and she'd probably be more upset than she already was if she knew that the Fillies had guessed. There was no question about it anymore—Matt had decided to sell Webster's, and Emily's worst fears had come true.

She rolled over and punched her pillow, which felt as if it was filled with rocks, and tried to find a comfortable position. Trouble was troubling her, all right, but there was nothing she could do about it tonight. Tomorrow, however, Emily decided to call a council of war. It was up to the Fillies to save Webster's, and among the seven of them, they were sure to come up with a plan.

Other books in the **HORSE CRAZY** series:

HORSE PLAY

by Virginia Vail

Illustrated by Daniel Bodé

Troll Associates

Library of Congress Cataloging-in-Publication Data

Vail, Virginia.
    Horse play / by Virginia Vail; illustrated by Daniel Bode.
      p.   cm.—(Horse crazy ; #5)
    Summary: Thirteen-year-old Emily and her fellow campers at
Webster's Country Horse Camp fear that the owner plans to sell his
land to a real estate developer, so they stretch the truth a bit in
trying to convince the developer of imaginary hazards on the
property.
    ISBN 0-8167-1659-5 (lib. bdg.)   ISBN 0-8167-1660-9 (pbk.)
    [1. Camps—Fiction. 2. Horses—Fiction.] I. Bode, Daniel, ill.
II. Title. III. Series: Vail, Virginia. Horse crazy ; #5.
PZ7.V192Ho 1990
[Fic]—dc19   89-31347

A TROLL BOOK, published by Troll Associates,
Mahwah, NJ 07430

10 9 8 7 6 5 4 3 2 1

Chapter One

"Listen to this," Lynda Graves said, looking up from the sheet of paper on which she'd been writing. She picked up the paper and read aloud: " 'I have been coming to Webster's Country Horse Camp since I was a ten-year-old Foal. Now I'm a fourteen-year-old Filly, and I can't wait to come back next year, when I'll be a Thoroughbred. Webster's is the greatest camp in the world for girls who love horses. I'd be glad to tell other girls about it. Please write to me and I promise to write back.' How's that?"

The rest of the Fillies smiled at her.

"That's terrific, Lynda," Emily Jordan said. "I bet Matt and Marie will use it when they send out information to girls who are thinking of coming to Webster's next year."

Matt and Marie Webster, who owned and ran the camp, had asked all the campers to write short notes about Webster's. The best ones would be included with the brochure they sent out each year. Foals, Fil-

1

lies, and Thoros were gathered in the Activity Room on this August afternoon, busily writing.

"What did you write, Emily?" asked Penny Marshall, one of the youngest Fillies. "Read it to us."

"Well . . ." Emily felt herself blushing. "I don't think Matt and Marie will choose mine. I keep trying to make it general, but all I can talk about is Joker!"

"Oh, we know you're in love with that palomino," Caroline Lescaux said, laughing. "But you don't want to make him sound *too* good, or everybody will want him to be their special horse for the summer."

Emily ran her fingers through her short brown hair and sighed. "Yeah, I know. And if somebody else gets Joker next summer, I'll absolutely *die!*"

"Matt wouldn't give him to anybody but you," Libby Dexter assured her, "just like he wouldn't give Foxy to anybody but me. And he wouldn't *dare* give Dan to anybody but Lynda. Old campers get first dibs."

"Want to hear what I wrote?" Danny Franciscus asked, her dark eyes sparkling.

"Sure," Emily said, glad to be off the hook. "Read it to us, Danny."

Danny stood up, cleared her throat, and began to read from the paper she held in her hand. " 'Every girl who has ever dreamed of having her own horse should definitely come to Webster's Country Horse Camp. Here in the midst of the Adirondacks in upper New York State, surrounded by the beauties of nature, each girl has a horse assigned to her for the entire six-week season, a horse that nobody else

2

rides but her. She develops a personal relationship with her horse, just like Velvet Brown and The Pie in that wonderful book, *National Velvet,* that was made into a movie with Elizabeth Taylor and . . .' "

"Uh . . . that's awfully long, Danny," Pam Webster interrupted. She was the Fillies' counselor as well as Matt and Marie's only daughter. "We don't have a whole lot of room to print these letters. Maybe you ought to cut it down a little. But it's really good," she added, as Danny's face fell.

Penny nudged Dru Carpenter, her best friend at Webster's and twelve years old, like herself. "Dru, read yours," she urged.

"Oh, I don't know . . ." Dru mumbled through her braces. She was a little overweight—but only a little—because she'd been dieting over the summer, and she was a lot slimmer than when she'd first arrived.

"Read it, Dru," Emily suggested.

"Well, okay, but it's not very good." Dru picked up her paper and glanced shyly at the other Fillies. "I said . . . well, this is what I said. 'When I came to Webster's Country Horse Camp, I was kind of afraid of horses because they were so big and I didn't know how to ride, but everybody was so nice to me, and they taught me how to ride and how to not be afraid of horses, so now I'm not afraid of horses at all, and my horse, Donna, is my best friend, and she's not afraid of me and I'm not afraid of her and I want to come back next year and I hope if you're scared of horses you'll come too because

3

after you've been at Webster's for a while you won't be, either.' " She looked at Pam. "That's pretty long, too. I just didn't know how to stop."

"It's just fine, Dru," Pam said. "You're right—it is a bit long, but you can cut it." She glanced at her watch. "You campers have five more minutes. Finish up, and I'll give your papers to Mom and Dad. And when I've handed them in, I'll meet you at the stables so we can saddle up and go on a trail ride with the Foals and Thoros."

Emily bent over her paper, crossing out most of what she'd written and trying to squeeze everything she felt about Webster's into a few short sentences. It wasn't easy. How could she possibly tell anyone how neat it was, and how beautiful the horses were, and what nice people the Websters were?

Being at Webster's is like becoming part of a big, happy family, she wrote. *And the best part is, the Websters love horses just as much as I do.* She nibbled at the eraser on her pencil, remembering how she almost hadn't come to camp at all when her best friend, Judy Bradford, broke her leg. They'd been planning on spending the summer at Webster's together, and Emily had been afraid she'd be lonely and homesick without Judy. But Judy had persuaded her to come anyway, and Emily was awfully glad she had! *Don't worry about being lonely,* she scribbled. *All the girls are really friendly, and there are all kinds of fun things to do, like trail rides, and camping out, and horse shows. Even if you're not a very good rider at first, you will be by the end of the summer.*

Emily had been afraid she'd be the worst rider at camp, but she wasn't. And she'd learned so much over the past four weeks that she had actually won two ribbons on Field Day. Four weeks! Emily could hardly believe that there were only two more weeks of the camp season to go. She hated the thought of saying good-bye to her beloved Joker. She'd be counting the days until she and Judy came back to Webster's next summer.

If you want to know more about Webster's, please write or phone me, she wrote, then added her name, address, and telephone number.

"Time's up," Pam said. Emily handed over her paper along with everyone else. She hoped Matt and Marie would choose hers to be in their brochure. It would be fun to hear from girls who were thinking about coming to Webster's, because they would all be horse crazy, just like she was. They'd have a lot in common. Emily had never had a pen pal, but she was looking forward to having one now.

Little red-haired Libby, who was the same age as Emily—thirteen—but much shorter, caught up with her as she left the Activity Room.

"Hey, Emily, I wrote one of those letters last year," Libby said. "And it went out with the brochure. How come you never called me, or wrote to me?"

Emily shrugged. "I guess I was kind of shy. I felt funny about writing to somebody I didn't know at all. But I'm not shy anymore." She grinned at Libby, who was her closest friend at Webster's. "I wish I had written to you! Then I would have known that you're a nut!"

"Me? A nut? Just because I want to be a jockey?" Libby said, pretending to be annoyed.

"No, *not* because you want to be a jockey!" Emily replied, laughing. "Just because you're a plain, ordinary nut!"

"I resemble that remark," Libby said, laughing too.

"What's so funny?" asked Caro Lescaux, joining Emily and Libby as they headed for the stables. Instead of wearing her usual outfit of elegant, expensive riding clothes, Caro had on a green T-shirt with WEBSTER'S COUNTRY HORSE CAMP in big white letters across the chest, and faded jeans. Her silky blond hair was pulled back in a ponytail, and she wasn't wearing any makeup at all. Emily knew why: Caro had flipped out over Emily's older brother, Eric, when he had visited the camp just last week with Emily's parents and her best friend Judy. Caro had been a different girl ever since. Instead of bragging about how rich her folks were and acting like such a snob that the other Fillies called her Princess Caro, she was actually being nice to everybody, and especially to Emily. And she'd stopped wearing lots of makeup because Eric had told her he didn't like it. But that was the *only* thing Eric didn't like about Caro. The whole time he was at Webster's, he'd walked around with a goofy grin on his face, and the grin got even goofier every time he set eyes on Caro.

6

"Nothing, really," Emily said now in answer to Caro's question. "We were just kidding around."

"Uh . . . I don't suppose you've heard anything from your parents, or Judy, or . . . anybody, have you?" Caro asked casually.

" 'Anybody' meaning Eric?" Libby teased. Emily wasn't the only Filly who had noticed how dopey Caro and Eric had been acting.

"They only went home yesterday, Caro," Emily pointed out. "Unless they'd sent a telegram or something, I couldn't possibly have heard from them so soon."

"Well, I just thought they might have called to let you know they got home all right," Caro said. She glanced at Libby, who had picked up some pine-cones from under the trees and was trying to juggle three of them as she walked along. Lowering her voice, Caro said, "Emily, could I talk to you a minute?"

"Sure. Talk," Emily said cheerfully.

"Privately," Caro whispered, glancing at Libby again.

Wondering what she had to say that Libby couldn't hear, Emily said, "Okay. I have to pick up my riding hat from the cabin. Want to come along?"

Caro nodded, and Emily called to Libby, "Caro and I are making a detour to the cabin. See you at the stables, okay?"

"Okay . . . *drat*!" Libby dropped a pinecone. "Now I have to start all over again!"

7

"What's up?" Emily asked as she and Caro headed for the Fillies' bunkhouse.

"Well . . ." Caro seemed to be having trouble getting the words out, and that wasn't like Caro— at least, not like the *old* Caro. She'd always had plenty to say, even if it was something the person she was talking to didn't want to hear.

Remembering the game of charades the campers had played the other night around the campfire, Emily tugged at her earlobe and said, "Sounds like?" Then she made a big circle with her arms. "How about the whole thing?"

Caro giggled. "Oh, stop it!" But then she got serious again. "You remember what I told you when we were grooming our horses on Friday?"

Emily remembered, all right. She hadn't been able to believe her ears when Caro had confessed that her family wasn't really wealthy, like she'd said, and that her "princess" act had been exactly that— an act. Emily nodded.

"You . . . uh . . . you didn't tell anybody else, did you?" Caro asked.

"Nobody except Judy," Emily told her. "And I'm sure Judy didn't tell anybody, either. Why? What does it matter?" She pushed open the screen door to the cabin and went over to the camp trunk at the foot of her bunk to get her velvet-covered hard hat.

"I'm not sure, exactly," Caro admitted. "It's just that . . . well, I mean . . ." She stared down at the floor, biting her lower lip.

Since Caro was still having a hard time putting her

9

thoughts into words, Emily glanced around the cabin and saw Caro's hard hat on her bunk. She went over and picked it up, then tossed it at Caro.

"Here . . . catch!"

"Gee, thanks," Caro said, catching the hat and jamming it on her head. "I completely forgot that I left mine here, too." Emily noticed that Caro didn't check out her appearance in the mirror. She had changed, all right!

Then Emily noticed something else. On the wall where the Fillies had tacked up a lot of photographs that Emily had taken of them and their horses, there was a bare spot. Emily went over to take a closer look and saw that the missing photo was one she'd taken of Caro with Dark Victory, the big bay she'd been assigned for the summer.

"Hey, Caro," she said, "look. Your picture's gone. I wonder what happened to it. Maybe it fell on the floor."

She was bending down to search for it when she heard Caro say, "It didn't fall down. I took it."

"Well, put it back, okay? We have everybody here except you . . . even Judy." Emily couldn't help smiling at Judy's photo. It was a close-up shot because Judy hadn't wanted to have her cast in the picture, and Judy had crossed one eye just as Emily had pressed the button. Boy, did she look silly!

"I can't put it back because I don't have it anymore," Caro told her, blushing.

"What did you do with it?" Emily asked. "You didn't tear it up or anything, did you?" She knew

10

how picky Caro was when it came to pictures of herself. If she didn't look absolutely perfect, like a model in a fashion magazine, she had a fit. "That was a *good* picture. You looked great."

"I know," Caro said. "And I didn't tear it up. I mailed it."

"Mailed it?" Emily repeated. "Who did you . . ." And then light dawned. "Oh, I get it. You sent it to Eric, right?"

Caro smiled, but her face was still pink. "He asked me if I had a picture he could have, and I said I didn't. And then after he left, I remembered that one, so when I wrote him a letter last night, I sent him the photo, too. You can take another one to add to the collection."

"Okay, I will," Emily said, wondering where Eric would put the picture of Caro. Next to the photo of his high-school football team? She still couldn't quite get used to the thought of her big brother having a girlfriend, even a long-distance one, like Caro. Then she glanced at her watch. "Hey, we'd better get moving, or they'll start the trail ride without us!"

"What I was trying to say before," Caro said as they left the bunkhouse and trotted toward the stables, "is that I wish you wouldn't tell the other girls what I told you on Friday. I'd really feel like a jerk if they knew that I've been pretending to be somebody I'm not. I mean, if I'm not who I said I was, then who *am* I?"

Emily swung her riding hat from its chin strap, thinking about that for a few minutes. At last she

11

said, "You're *you,* Caro Lescaux, a Filly at Webster's, just like the rest of us. What's so terrible about that?"

"Nothing, I guess." Caro looked over at Emily almost shyly. "But I wish you wouldn't tell them anyway. I will if I have to, but only if I *have* to, okay?"

Emily shrugged. "Whatever you say. But I don't think Eric would like knowing you're trying to pass yourself off as a snob!"

"That's not what I mean!" Caro sighed. "I don't want to pass myself off as a snob. From now on, I'm going to try *not* to act like a snob. I want to be friends with you and the other Fillies, so when we all come back to Webster's next summer, I won't be an outsider anymore. I really love it here!"

"I do, too," Emily said. "And the only reason you're an outsider is because we all thought you wanted it that way. I won't say anything to anybody else, Caro, unless . . ."

"Unless?"

"Unless you start acting like you used to—putting everybody down and getting out of chores and stuff like that," Emily said sternly.

"I won't. At least, I'll try not to." Caro grinned. "And if I do, I give you permission to tell me when I'm becoming a pain in the neck."

Emily laughed. "Is that a promise?"

"That's a promise," Caro said solemnly. She stuck out her hand, and Emily shook it. "Friends?" Caro asked.

"Friends," Emily replied. "Maybe you could

12

come and visit us sometime over the winter. I bet Eric would like that."

Caro fluttered her long lashes. "I'd like that, too. As a matter of fact, Eric already mentioned it."

"I'm not surprised," Emily said. "Hurry up! I can see Rachel and the Thoros coming into the stable yard right now!"

Chapter Two

"Where are we going, Rachel?" Lynda asked as she trotted up to the Thoros' counselor on her dapple-gray gelding, the Dandy. Rachel was leading the trail ride and Pam was bringing up the rear, keeping an eye on any stragglers as the campers rode along the bridle path beside the Winnepac River. Emily and Caro had just barely managed to saddle up their horses and join the others before they left, and now Joker and Vic had taken their places between Foxy, Libby's mount, and Pepper, Penny's horse.

"I thought we'd just follow the river for a while," Rachel said. "We'll go down to the shallows and cross over to Palmer's Island, then take the bridge back to shore."

"Sounds good." Lynda waited until the Thoros had passed, then fell into line behind Danny.

"Maybe we'll run into some of the Long Branch boys," Danny said. "I bet they ride along the river sometimes, too." Long Branch was the boys' camp

14

across the Winnepac River, and the Long Branch campers had competed against Webster's campers on Field Day.

"I hope we don't run into anybody," Dru said, bouncing along contentedly on Donna, her plump little mare. "I like it being just us. It's so neat out here with no houses and no people—just horses and trees and sunshine."

Her voice drifted back to Emily, and she couldn't have agreed more. Emily envied Pam, her brothers, Warren and Chris, and their parents living here all year round. Chris, Pam's younger brother, who was only a year older than Emily, had told her about how beautiful it was here in the Adirondacks in winter, when the snow was so deep that sometimes the school bus couldn't make it up the road to the farmhouse. And she could imagine how glorious the fall foliage must be in September. Emily had never really thought about what she wanted to do when she grew up, except that it had to be something to do with horses. Wouldn't it be neat if she and Judy could buy a farm some day and start a camp just like Webster's? Just the two of them in the wilderness, with lots of wonderful horses—and maybe Libby, when she wasn't riding in some race somewhere. . . .

"Who's that?"

Libby's voice interrupted her thoughts, and Emily blinked. "Who's what?" she asked.

"That funny-looking man in the suit, up there by the sheep pasture with Matt."

Emily looked where Libby was pointing. Sure enough, she saw Matt Webster and another man, and the other man was indeed wearing a suit. It wasn't so much his suit that was funny-looking but that he was wearing it in a field instead of in an office. He seemed to be showing Matt some big papers, and he was making large, sweeping gestures while Matt nodded and looked at the papers.

"Beats me," Emily said. "Maybe he's somebody who wants to buy some wool." She knew that Marie Webster spun yarn from the wool of their sheep, then knitted it into beautiful sweaters and sold them.

"Maybe," Libby said. "But he doesn't look like a sheep person. He looks . . . *suspicious.*"

"Suspicious?" Caro echoed from behind Emily. "Come on, Libby! Do you think he has a gun in his pocket or something? He just looks like a plain, ordinary businessman to me."

"I know what Libby means," Danny offered, turning in her saddle to look at the two men. "Not suspicious like somebody who'd carry a gun, but like somebody who doesn't belong here. I don't like him at all. He has shifty eyes!"

Everybody who could hear her burst into laughter.

"You can't even *see* his eyes from here, Danny," Lynda said. "You don't even know if he *has* eyes!"

Danny reached down to stroke Misty, her mount, and said stubbornly, "Of course he has eyes, Lynda, and maybe I can't exactly see them, but I bet they're

17

shifty, anyway. People who wear business suits way out in the country *always* have shifty eyes."

"What do you suppose he's showing Matt?" Penny asked. "Those papers are really big—like ground plans, or something. Maybe blueprints. My dad's an architect, and he's always waving papers like that around."

"Maybe Matt wants to build a fancy house for the sheep," Dru suggested. "So they don't get cold in the winter."

"Let's ask Pam when we get back," Lynda suggested. "I bet she knows what's going on."

"Look!" shouted one of the Foals. "Up in the sky—see all those birds?"

All the girls looked up and saw the birds high overhead, flying in a perfect V formation.

"What kind of birds are they, Pam?" another Foal asked.

"Canada geese," Pam said. "They're flying south because they know the cold weather's coming."

"I wonder *how* they know," Penny mused aloud. "And how do they know to fly together like that?"

"And how do they know which way is south?" Dru said. "I wouldn't know unless I had a compass or something."

The campers had reined their horses to a halt, watching the geese until they disappeared from sight.

"Let's go, gang," Rachel called, clucking to her horse and urging him forward. The others followed.

Emily sighed and patted Joker's satiny golden

18

shoulder. She spoke very softly, so only he could hear. "Seeing those geese made me kind of sad, Joker. It means that the summer's almost over, and then I won't see you again for almost a whole year! But you won't forget me, will you? I'll be thinking about you all the time."

Joker's ears flicked back and forth, so she knew he was listening to her.

"I don't think I could stand it if I didn't know I was coming back to Webster's next summer," she told him. "But I am, and so is Judy. And you'll be my horse again, just like you are now."

To Emily's delight, Joker nodded his head and snorted as though he not only heard, but understood. And no matter what anybody said, she was sure he did. Besides being the most beautiful horse in the world, Emily knew he was the most intelligent.

Rachel's horse, Daffy, began to trot. The rest of the horses picked up their pace as well, and Emily posted effortlessly to Joker's smooth gait. She didn't even have to think about it anymore—it was as natural as breathing—raising and lowering herself in rhythm, gripping with her knees and calves, the way Pam had taught her. The bridle path was very close to the riverbank now, and the afternoon sun filtered down through the leaves of the trees and glinted on the brown water of the Winnepac. Looking out over the water, Emily could see a lot of brightly colored sails as about a dozen small boats, propelled by a gentle breeze, skimmed over the waves.

19

"Looks like the Long Branch boys are having a sailboat race," Libby called over her shoulder.

"The blue-and-white striped boat is winning," Caro said from behind Emily. Then, "Whoops—no, it's not. That one with the rainbow sail is passing it! Wow, look at him go!"

Emily felt sorry for the blue-and-white striped one, so she yelled, "C'mon, blue-and-white!"

"Come on, rainbow!" Caro shouted.

All the campers slowed their horses to a walk, taking sides and cheering for one boat or the other. Their shrill voices were the only sound on the quiet afternoon air, and Emily could see the boy in the boat with the blue-and-white sail waving for a second. She wondered if he was one of the boys who had competed with Webster's girls on Field Day. If he was, he was much better at sailing than he'd been at riding—Webster's had creamed Long Branch in the riding competition. But then, according to Libby and Lynda, they always did. Long Branch wasn't a horse camp, like Webster's, and the boys didn't concentrate on riding the way campers at Webster's did.

"Move it, campers," Rachel called. "At this rate we'll never make it to the island and back in time for supper." She urged Daffy into a canter, and the other riders began to canter, too. They soon left the sailboats far behind, and everybody, including Emily, forgot about Long Branch, the Canada geese, and the strange man in the business suit back by the sheep pasture.

*   *   *

"If I never see another squash again, it'll be too soon," Caro grumbled a few hours later. The Fillies were on garden detail, and the vegetables they had been told to pick were tomatoes, corn, and . . . squash. Zucchini and yellow summer squash covered the vines everywhere they looked.

"Don't you like Marie's Italian squash with tomatoes and garlic?" Danny asked, tossing a slender green zucchini into the basket Emily was holding. "And what about her squash fritters? They're my favorite."

"I liked them the first time she made them," Caro sighed. "But day after day after day . . ."

"I love Marie's zucchini bread with raisins and walnuts," Emily said. "That doesn't taste like squash at all."

"But I *know* it's squash," Caro said. "Lately I think Marie puts squash in everything—I'm getting squashed out!"

"That's the way it is on a farm," Lynda said cheerfully. "When vegetables are in season, you sell as much as you can, eat as much as you can, and freeze or preserve the rest." She checked Emily's basket with a critical eye. "I think we have enough now, added to what Penny and Dru have picked. Marie told me she's going to try something new—squash brownies!"

"You *are* kidding, aren't you?" Caro groaned. "Squash *brownies*?"

"That's what she said," Lynda told her. "It's a

21

recipe she made up. She's going to call them 'squashies.' "

"I think squash brownies sound good," Dru put in. "I bet they'll be lots lower in calories than regular brownies, and that's important when you're watching your weight, like I am." Dru looked so much better now that she was slimmer. And when she was smiling, as she was now, she didn't try to hide her braces anymore. She was a very different Filly from the shy, unhappy girl she once was.

"Corn next," Lynda said, leading the way out of the squash patch to the cornfield.

"I just *love* corn," Danny exclaimed. "And Webster's corn is the best I ever tasted."

"It's not bad," Lynda said. "It's almost as good as the corn we grow back on the farm in Iowa. Marie's going to make corn fritters for supper."

"Good!" Dru pulled off an ear and dropped it in the bushel basket at her feet. "I can't eat corn on the cob because it gets stuck in my braces, but I can handle fritters."

Libby, who had been filling her basket with tomatoes, came over and joined the rest of the Fillies in the cornfield. "My grandmother says the best way to eat corn is to build a fire and boil a pot of water right next to the corn stalk and drop the ears in the minute you pick and husk them. The longer you wait, the starchier they get."

Caro suddenly gave a screech. *"Yuck!* There's a big, fat, ugly *worm* on this one!"

Emily laughed. "That just goes to show that the

22

worms know what's good—they don't even wait to build a fire before they dig in!"

"Very funny," Caro said, making a face. "If he's enjoying it so much, I'll let him have it."

"Hey, Caro, where's your sense of adventure?" Libby tossed a couple of ears into the basket. "Don't you want to try Marie's worm fritters? They're the greatest!"

Caro sniffed. "Libby, you have a warped sense of humor."

As the girls traded jokes and insults, Emily wandered down the rows of corn, picking the fattest, juiciest-looking ears and tucking one or two tiny ones into the pocket of her jeans. She'd give them to Joker later, as a special treat. He certainly deserved them more than some yucky worm!

Emily paused for a moment, looking up at the late afternoon sky. There were a few soft, fleecy clouds—kind of like the Websters' sheep—floating overhead, and she was reminded all of a sudden of the man in the business suit. She wondered if anybody had found out who he was. Lynda was going to ask Pam about him, but Emily doubted if she'd had time yet. Not that it really mattered. It was just that he seemed so out of place somehow— suspicious, like Libby had said. But Libby had a powerful imagination. Still, it wouldn't hurt to find out who he was and what he was doing there. . . .

"Emily? Emily, where are you? It's time to go back to the farmhouse."

Lynda's voice interrupted Emily's thoughts, and

she hurried back between the rows of tall stalks, clutching the ears she'd picked in her arms. She could almost taste those fritters now, drenched in luscious maple syrup!

As the Fillies started for the farmhouse, lugging their baskets of vegetables, Penny asked, "How come some of the tomatoes and squash have bites taken out of them? Worms don't do that, do they?"

Lynda, the expert on farm produce, said, "No. Those bites aren't from worms. Worms don't have teeth! They're from raccoons or deer. They just love to munch on fresh veggies."

"And they love to knock over the garbage cans, too, and eat everything they can find," Danny said. "Marie's always saying how it's almost impossible to keep them away from food. The raccoons can even pry off the garbage can lids with their little hands."

"Paws," Caro corrected. "*People* have hands—raccoons have paws."

Danny shrugged. "Whatever. But they're awfully cute."

"I'd like to have a little raccoon for a pet," Dru said. "I love their little masks and their funny striped tails."

"But raccoons have rabies sometimes, like mad dogs," Lynda said. "You have to be very careful around them."

"Deer don't have rabies," Danny said. "They're just pretty and graceful and sweet—like Bambi. Are there lots of deer around here?"

Lynda nodded. "Lots. They're becoming a problem because they aren't as afraid of people as they used to be. And they seem to know that they're perfectly safe until hunting season begins."

Emily shuddered. "I *hate* the thought of people shooting those defenseless deer! It's not fair—the deer can't fight back."

"I had venison once. It was pretty good," Caro said.

"Caro!" Danny cried. "You might have eaten Bambi!"

"It was only once," Caro murmured. "I mean, it's not like I ate Bambiburgers every day for lunch!"

"Enough already," Lynda sighed. "Come on, gang. Bring your baskets into the kitchen, or else supper's going to be very late. And I don't know about you, but I'm so hungry after that trail ride that even a Bambiburger sounds good to me!"

Chapter Three

That evening between supper and campfire, the Fillies were lounging around the bunkhouse reading, writing letters home, or just resting. Everyone was pretty tired from the long trail ride on top of their morning riding classes, swimming, volleyball, and their garden chores. But it was a nice kind of tired, Emily thought as she took out her brand new pad of camp stationery. She'd used up all the paper she'd brought from home writing to her family, her grandparents, and most of all, to Judy. She'd promised to tell Judy everything that happened at Webster's so Judy would feel that she was there, too, and she'd hardly missed a day.

She looked down at the stationery and smiled. It was white, with the figure of a horse and WEBSTER'S COUNTRY HORSE CAMP printed in green at the top. She'd bought a green pen at the camp store, too, and now she took off the cap and began to write.

Dear Judy,

This afternoon the Foals, Thoros, and Fillies went on a trail ride together, with Rachel and Pam. We went right along the river, all the way to Palmer's Island and back. I didn't have time to show you the island when you were here, but it's really neat. Hardly anybody ever goes there, and it's kind of like a wildlife sanctuary. The animals and birds weren't afraid of us or anything.

And you know what? I was thinking today that what I want to do when we're both grown up and finished with college and everything is to start a camp just like Webster's! We could ride all day long, and teach kids to ride the way the Websters do. Then we could live in the country all year round, just us and the horses, and the kids in the summertime. What do you think we should call our camp?

Emily paused, putting down her pen. They'd have to think up a really good name—something like Horse Haven, or maybe . . .

"Pam, who was that man talking to Matt today?"

Penny's voice interrupted Emily's thoughts. She looked up from where she was sitting on her bunk and saw Pam put down the riding boot she was polishing.

"What man?" Pam asked, puzzled.

"You know, the one in the business suit with all the papers over by the sheep pasture," Dru said. "Is

27

Matt going to build a nice warm house for the sheep so they don't get cold during the winter?"

Pam frowned. "Oh, you mean Mr. Frick." But she didn't say anything else.

"Who's Mr. Frick?" Danny asked, laying down the book she had been reading. "Is he a friend of Matt's?"

Pam shrugged. "I wouldn't exactly call him a friend."

"Is he an *enemy* then?" Libby leaped down from the bunk over Emily's, landing on her feet as silently as a cat, and went over to sit down beside Pam on her cot. "He looked like a suspicious character to me!"

"Libby, you've been watching too much TV," Pam said, laughing. "Mr. Frick isn't a suspicious character, and he's not an enemy, either. He's just a business acquaintance of Dad's."

"What kind of business?" Lynda asked. "He sure didn't look like a horse person."

"He's not." Pam picked up her other boot and began polishing it vigorously. "He's a land developer."

"What's a land developer?" Dru wanted to know.

Pam glanced at her. "Hey, what is this? Twenty questions? A land developer is somebody who buys property and builds things on it. Then he sells it to somebody else for big bucks."

Penny asked, "What kind of things does he build? Houses?"

"Fourteen questions to go," Pam said. "Or

28

maybe thirteen—I lost count. Yes, he builds houses and stores and office buildings."

"So what was he doing here today?"

Pam shrugged again. "Search me, Caro. Maybe he's still trying to persuade Dad to sell the farm. Mr. Frick has been after him for years."

Emily forgot all about her letter to Judy. "He wants Matt to sell *Webster's*?"

"That's right." Pam held up her boot, examining it critically. "He wants to buy our land so he can build vacation homes on our property, with a swimming pool and a marina and a little shopping center and stuff like that."

She had everybody's attention now. All the Fillies stared at her, unable to believe their ears.

"Here?" Emily squawked. "Right *here*? He wants to tear down the cabins and the stables and get rid of the horses and put up *houses*?"

"And a *shopping center*?" Danny gasped.

"That's what he'd like to do," Pam said.

"That's crazy!" Lynda cried. "Who'd pay a lot of money for a house way out here? Webster's is in the middle of nowhere! There's nothing here except grass and trees—"

"And horses," Emily added.

"It's not all that crazy," Pam said. "Mr. Frick figures that because our property is so unspoiled, city people will want to move right in."

"And spoil it!" Danny said. "They'd pollute the water and the air, and drive the wild animals away.

30

And then it would be just like the city, and they wouldn't want it anymore."

"Matt's not going to sell, is he?" Penny asked.

"Of course not," Libby said. "Why would he want to do a dumb thing like that? Matt would never sell Webster's. . . ." She glanced at Pam. "Would he?"

"Well, he was kind of tempted for a while," Pam admitted. "We're a pretty expensive family, you know. I'm going to be a sophomore in college this fall, and Warren will be going to college next year, so that'll be two tuitions to pay. And then there'll be Chris in a few years . . . and the horses cost an awful lot to feed and care for."

"But horses are Matt's whole *life*," Emily said.

Pam smiled. "Mine, too. We're all just as crazy about horses as you are, Emily, and that's why Dad didn't sell, even though we're always hurting for money."

"Money isn't everything."

All the Fillies stared at Caro.

"I can't believe you just said that!" Lynda exclaimed. "I thought money was where it's at as far as you're concerned."

Caro tossed her sleek blond head. "Well then, I guess you don't know me very well. I'm not saying money isn't important, just that it's not *everything*. And when it comes to Webster's . . ."

"When it comes to Webster's, you've always acted as if you didn't want to be here because it's not one of those expensive horse camps where everybody's parents are millionaires like your folks," Libby said.

"I never said my folks were millionaires," Caro muttered, glancing at Emily, who didn't have the slightest idea of what to say. She'd promised Caro she wouldn't tell the rest of the Fillies that Caro's family wasn't rich at all, and so far, she hadn't. Did Caro want her to tell the truth now?

Before she could decide what to do, Penny spoke. "It doesn't matter how much money Caro's parents have," she said softly, twisting the end of one blond braid. "What *does* matter is what's going to happen to Webster's. If Matt sells the land, there won't be any more horse camp, will there?"

Pam had finished polishing her second boot, and now she set it down neatly next to the other one. Smiling, she said, "Hey, don't get all bent out of shape, okay? I told you Dad was *tempted* to sell, but that was years ago. I don't know what Mr. Frick was doing here today, but I *do* know that Dad wouldn't make a deal with him without discussing it first with Mom, Warren, Chris, and me. And he hasn't, so that's that! I shouldn't have told you about it anyway. Let's forget it, all right?" She stood up and looked at her watch. "Come on, Fillies, let's get moving. Campfire is going to begin in a few minutes, and we don't want to be late."

But Emily couldn't forget it, and neither could her bunkmates. As they obediently trooped out of the cabin, heading for the picnic grove, everybody was whispering worriedly.

"Matt and Marie wouldn't sell out. They couldn't!"

"You're right, Lynda. If they were even thinking about selling, they wouldn't have asked us to write those letters about how great the camp is," Libby said.

"And Pam said she was sure Matt wouldn't do anything without telling his family about it," Penny added.

"But what if Mr. Frick made Matt an offer he couldn't refuse, and he hasn't told anybody yet?" Emily murmured.

"I *knew* that man looked suspicious!" Libby said grimly.

Suddenly Danny stopped in her tracks. "I just had a terrible thought!" she cried. "What if there's a big mortgage on the farm, and Matt can't pay it off, and the bank is going to foreclose, and he *has* to sell? That's exactly what happened in a book I read once. This family lost *everything* when the bank foreclosed on their farm. They had to move to the city and start all over again, and they were awfully poor. And the *worst* part was when the man who bought the farm *shot* Mindy's horse—Mindy was the heroine. I cried so much I could hardly finish the book!"

Emily shuddered. In her mind's eye, she could see Mr. Frick in his business suit lining up all Webster's horses and picking them off one by one. And when he came to Joker . . . her eyes filled with tears. "I don't even want to think about it!" she whispered.

"If Matt sells, what will happen to the horses, and the sheep, and the little lambs?" Dru quavered.

"Vacation homes, and a shopping center! I can't stand it!" Lynda said.

Even though the sunset sky was glowing orange and pink, none of the Fillies noticed it. They didn't hear the voices of the Thoros and Foals as they sang merrily around the fire:

"I had a cat and the cat pleased me,
I fed my cat under yonder tree.
Cat goes fiddle-ee-fee!
I had a hen and the hen pleased me.
I fed my hen under yonder tree.
Hen goes chimmy-chuck, chimmy-chuck,
Cat goes fiddle-ee-fee. . . ."

If there's not going to be any Webster's next summer, nothing's *going to please me,* Emily thought sadly as the words of the song finally sank in. If Matt and Marie sold their property, there wouldn't be any more campfires or riding lessons or trail rides or horse shows. There wouldn't be any *horses*! And what about Joker? What would happen to him? She didn't really think Mr. Frick would shoot him, but Joker would probably be sold with the rest of the horses, and she'd never see him again.

Emily grabbed Libby's arm. "We can't let him do it!" she said. "We have to think of some way to stop Matt from selling Webster's!"

"Take it easy, Emily," Libby said. "We don't *know* that Matt's going to sell. Like my grandmother says, don't trouble trouble till trouble troubles you."

34

Emily frowned. Sometimes the things Libby's gram said were a little hard to understand. "What does that mean?" she asked.

"It means that there's no point in getting all upset about something bad that hasn't happened yet and maybe won't happen at all," Libby told her. "And I'm absolutely positive that Matt won't sell the farm." She paused, then added, "But if he changes his mind, you're right—we have to find a way to stop him."

It was a very quiet little group of Fillies that took their places around the campfire. Penny and Dru huddled together side by side on a fallen log, looking as though they were about to burst into tears any minute, and none of the other Fillies looked much happier.

"What's the matter with you guys?" asked Meghan, one of the Thoros. "You look as though you've lost your last friend."

"Nothing's the matter," Lynda mumbled, staring glumly into the flames.

"Nothing at all," Danny sighed.

"Well, you could have fooled me," Meghan said. "If nothing's wrong, then cheer up! Rachel's organized a scavenger hunt. Go on over and get your list of the things the Fillies have to find. It's going to be fun! The Thoros, Foals, and Fillies each have to get as many things on their lists as they can, and the group that gets the most wins."

"And *we're* going to win," Janet, another Thoro, put in, smiling fiercely.

"Oh, really?" Caro perked up at the challenge. She couldn't resist competition. "Well, we'll just see about that! Come on, Fillies. Let's get our list."

Emily looked around the campfire. "Where's Pam? I thought she was going to meet us here."

"So did I," Lynda said, frowning. "Come to think of it, I don't see Marie, either, and she never misses campfire."

"And Warren and Chris aren't here." Penny's eyes widened. "Neither is Matt. You don't suppose . . ."

"A family conference!" Danny whispered. "I bet they're all at the farmhouse this very minute, and Matt's breaking the news to them about the mortgage and selling the farm, just like in that book!"

The girls looked at each other in dismay. Caro broke the silence. "What's the title of that book you keep talking about, Danny?"

Moving On," Danny said. "Why?"

"I just want to make sure I never, *ever* read it!" Caro told her.

"I don't feel much like playing games," Dru said in a small voice.

"Neither do I," Penny sighed. "If Matt's going to . . ."

"If Matt's going to what?" asked Janet, pausing beside the little group of Fillies.

Lynda jabbed Penny in the arm. "They don't know," she hissed in Penny's ear. "Nobody knows but us. Let's keep it that way for a while, okay? No sense in getting everybody else all depressed."

36

"Right," Emily agreed. "We have to act as if everything's perfectly normal." She swallowed the lump in her throat. In reply to Janet's question, she said, "We were just wondering if Matt's going to—uh—come to campfire later on."

"He probably will," Janet said cheerfully. "Aren't you going to pick up your list for the scavenger hunt?"

"Yeah . . . sure. Right away," Danny mumbled.

The Fillies trudged over to Rachel, who gave them each a copy of the list of things they would have to find.

"And you have to be back here in half an hour with all your stuff," she told them. "Then we'll see who's the winner."

"What's the prize?" Caro asked.

Rachel grinned. "You'll find out in half an hour. But you better get moving—the Thoros and the Foals are way ahead of you."

" 'One white athletic sock with a red-and-blue stripe,' " Lynda read aloud. "No problem! I have dozens of those."

" 'Three pinecones at least four inches long,' " Libby read. "Anybody got a ruler?"

"I know where there's a tiny blue flower—it's down by the sheep pasture," Dru said, brightening a little.

Caro studied her copy of the list. " 'A purple scarf'—I'm sure I have one of those. I probably have *six*!"

" 'A photograph of a good-looking guy,' " Emily

read. "I guess maybe that picture I have of my brother Eric would qualify."

"It sure would!" Caro purred.

The Fillies took off in different directions to pick up the items on their list. But as Emily headed for the Fillies' bunkhouse where her picture of Eric was thumbtacked over her bed, she wasn't happy. What difference did it make who won if Webster's was doomed? She and Judy would never make their dream of going to horse camp together come true. And even more important—most important of all—she'd lose Joker.

Emily thought about the big, beautiful palomino who'd been assigned to her for the summer. If Matt sold Webster's, some stranger would buy Joker, somebody who didn't care about him as Emily did. She remembered *Black Beauty,* one of her favorite books. What if Joker was sold to somebody who treated him badly? What if he was whipped and forced to haul heavy loads? What if nobody realized what a special, wonderful horse he was?

Then she gave herself a little shake. Maybe Libby was right. Maybe they were all jumping to conclusions. After all, just because Mr. Frick kept trying to talk Matt into selling his property, that didn't mean Matt was going to do it. And just because none of the Websters was at campfire didn't mean that they were talking about taking Mr. Frick up on his offer. They could be doing *anything*—watching TV or making plans for Sunday's horse show. . . .

Emily decided to take Gram's advice. Or at least, she was certainly going to try!

Chapter Four

After the Foals won the scavenger hunt and each proud little girl was given her prize—a big round button with I LOVE HORSES on it—Rachel and Melinda Willis, the Foals' counselor, let everyone help pop corn over the embers in old-fashioned, long-handled poppers. Then Melinda, who was the lead singer with Warren Webster's rock band, The River Rats, played Chris's guitar while all the campers sang. The Fillies didn't sing very loudly, though, and Emily hardly sang at all; she was too busy looking around to see if any of the Websters had shown up. When none of them did, Emily's spirits sank lower and lower.

They hit rock bottom back at the cabin as the girls were getting ready for bed. Pam came in, and the minute Emily saw her face, she knew something was very wrong. Pam's eyes were red, as though she had been crying, and her expression was sad.

"Are you okay, Pam?" Libby asked anxiously. "We missed you at campfire."

"We missed *all* of you," Danny added.

"Where were you, anyway?" Lynda asked.

Pam began undressing and putting on her pajamas. "I'm all right," she said. "We just got some bad news, and none of us felt much like coming to campfire tonight. Did Rachel and Melinda take care of everything?"

The Fillies assured her that they had. Then Emily said, "Uh, Pam, what kind of bad news?"

Getting into her cot and pulling the covers up to her chin, Pam said, "Family stuff." She looked around at the girls' concerned faces and smiled reassuringly. "Don't worry . . . everything's going to be all right . . . I hope."

"Is there anything we can do?" Dru asked.

"Anything you want to talk about?" Emily suggested.

Pam shook her head. "There's nothing I want to talk about, but there *is* something you can do."

Penny said, "What?"

"You can turn out the light. I'm pretty tired, and I bet you are, too. 'Night, Fillies. See you in the morning."

Long after the cabin was in darkness, Emily lay wide awake in her bunk. From the restless shifting and squirming above her, she knew that Libby couldn't sleep either. Emily wanted very much to talk to Libby, but she was afraid Pam might wake up and hear them. It was apparent that Pam didn't want anybody to know what the "bad news" was, and she'd probably be more upset than she already was if she knew that the Fillies had guessed. There was no question about it anymore—Matt had decided to sell Webster's, and Emily's worst fears had come true.

She rolled over and punched her pillow, which felt as if it was filled with rocks, and tried to find a comfortable position. Trouble was troubling her, all right, but there was nothing she could do about it tonight. Tomorrow, however, Emily decided to call a council of war. It was up to the Fillies to save Webster's, and among the seven of them, they were sure to come up with a plan.

While all the campers were mucking out their horses' stalls and grooming their mounts the next morning, Emily stuck her head into the stall next to Joker's where Caro was currying Dark Victory.

"Psst! Caro!" she whispered, glancing around to make sure none of the Websters was in earshot.

"What's up?" Caro asked.

"Plenty! We have to have a conference, all us Fillies, to figure out how to keep Matt from selling the camp," Emily told her in a low voice. "Let's meet over by the mares and foals' pasture right after lunch, okay? You tell Libby and Lynda during riding class, and I'll tell Penny, Danny, and Dru."

Caro nodded. "Good idea." She sighed. "I can't believe this is happening, just when I found out how much I love Webster's! I was really looking forward to coming back next summer."

"We all feel the same way, and I know the Foals

41

and Thoros do, too. But we mustn't tell them. Like Lynda said last night, there's no point in worrying everybody else—not yet, anyway."

Caro looked out over the door to Vic's stall, and her eyes widened. "Emily!" she whispered. "Look who's coming into the stable!"

Emily looked—and gasped. "Oh, no! It's Matt and Mr. Frick!"

Sure enough, the two men were walking slowly down the wide aisle between the rows of stalls, talking quietly. Mr. Frick's business suit looked even more out of place here than by the sheep pasture, Emily thought, scowling. Matt wasn't smiling, but Mr. Frick was.

"The nerve of him!" Emily muttered. "He doesn't own Webster's yet. He doesn't belong here!"

"Too bad none of the horses left a souvenir out there," Caro whispered. "I'd love to see those nice shiny shoes step right into a pile."

Both girls giggled in spite of themselves.

"The next time he comes around, we'll see if we can arrange it," Emily said. "If there *is* a next time, which I hope there isn't!"

"I wish we could have that conference right now," Caro said. "It looks as if Mr. Frick is planning on taking over sooner than we thought. We'll have to come up with a plan of attack fast."

Joker nudged Emily with his nose, reminding her that she had been neglecting him. She turned and put her arms around his neck.

"I haven't forgotten you," she assured him. "I'm thinking about you every single minute, believe me." Joker whuffled gently, stamping one hoof in the fresh straw she had spread on the floor of his stall. "I know—you're impatient to get out into the ring. Sorry I'm such a slowpoke this morning, but Caro and I had some important business to discuss." Emily gave the palomino one last affectionate pat, then took his pad and saddle and placed them on his sleek golden back. "It's about the future of Webster's, and your future, too," she told him, tightening the girth and cinching it. "You don't have anything to worry about, though. I won't let anything bad happen to you, I promise."

"Better not make promises you can't keep," Caro said as she saddled and bridled Vic.

Emily looked at her, surprised. "I thought you didn't believe horses understood when people talked to them."

"Well, maybe I've changed my mind." Caro fastened the throat latch on Vic's bridle. "Joker seems to understand what you say to him, and sometimes I think Vic does, too. But I don't think *all* horses do. Only the smart ones, like Vic and Joker."

Emily grinned. "Caro, you know something? You're not nearly as much of a pain as you used to be!"

"If that's a compliment, thanks," Caro said wryly. But she was grinning, too.

They led their horses out of their stalls, joining the rest of the campers who were heading for the three riding rings—beginners, intermediate, and advanced—where classes were held. Caro was in the advanced class with Libby and Lynda, and Emily, Danny, and Penny were Intermediates. Dru was the only Filly in the beginners' class, and as she and her little mare, Donna, passed Emily and Joker, Emily went over to her and said, "After lunch . . . down by the mares and foals. Meeting about you know what!"

Dru nodded solemnly. "I'll be there," she promised. "Did you see—"

"Matt and Mr. Frick? I sure did!"

Emily swung herself up into Joker's saddle. She looked over her shoulder, but the two men were nowhere to be seen. Matt was probably on his way to the advanced ring, where he taught the more experienced riders. But where was Mr. Frick? Probably snooping around somewhere, Emily thought, figuring out how he could tear down the stable and the indoor riding ring so he could build lots of tacky little houses that he could sell for thousands of dollars. Well, if that was what he was thinking, he had another think coming!

Emily tried very hard to concentrate on her riding lesson, but she couldn't help noticing that Pam, the intermediates' instructor, was having trouble concentrating, too. And no wonder. It must be breaking her heart, Emily thought, to know that once Mr. Frick owned the farm, her whole family would have

45

to move somewhere else and start a whole new life without the horses they all loved.

Emily managed to deliver her message about the meeting to Penny and Danny without any of the other intermediate riders hearing, and as soon as the class was over, the three of them ran up to the farmhouse, where they met Caro, Libby, Lynda, and Dru, and set the tables for lunch. Marie tried to be bright and cheerful, but she was obviously as worried as Pam had been as she set out the platters of sandwiches and bowls of salad. The Foals were scheduled to take care of cleanup and washing the dishes, so the Fillies would be free to leave as soon as they had finished eating.

"What's your hurry, Lynda?" Pam asked as Lynda gobbled up the last of her ham and cheese sandwich, snatched a peach from the bowl in the middle of the table, and stood up.

"Things to do. See you later," Lynda said quickly. "You coming, Libby?"

"Yep, right away!" Libby hurried after her. The rest of the Fillies began leaving, one by one.

"Where's everybody going in such a rush?" Pam asked Emily, the last to leave.

"Oh, nowhere. Just out," Emily said vaguely, tucking a few carrot sticks for Joker in her shirt pocket. She hesitated beside Pam's chair. "I guess it's not very polite to leave you here all by yourself. You don't mind, do you?"

Pam smiled. "No, I don't mind. And I'm not exactly all by myself, with all the Foals and Thoros around. You sure nothing's wrong, Emily? The Fillies have been acting kind of strange today."

"Strange?" Emily repeated. "Us? Gee, I don't think we're acting any stranger than usual."

"Hey, Emily, hurry up!" Danny called from the doorway.

"Gotta run," Emily said and dashed out the door.

A few minutes later, the girls were gathered under a tall tree next to the pasture where the mares and foals were kept. The mares calmly grazed while their offspring scampered around them on long, spindly legs. But this time, nobody climbed over the fence to join in their games. They had other, more important things on their minds.

Emily looked around to make sure no one was missing, then said, "Okay, we're all here. And we know *why* we're here." The others nodded solemnly. "Anybody got any ideas about how we can stop Matt from selling Webster's to Mr. Frick?"

Silence. Apparently nobody did.

"Don't *you* have any ideas, Emily? You're the one who called this meeting," Lynda said.

Emily sighed. "I called the meeting because I *don't* have any ideas," she confessed. "I was hoping somebody else did."

"Well . . ." Penny said, "the way I see it, what it comes down to is money. Mr. Frick must've offered Matt a lot of it to make him decide to sell. And if the Websters need money that badly, maybe we could find a way to offer him *more* if he *doesn't* sell."

"Oh, sure," Libby scoffed. "We all have pots of

47

money we don't know what to do with. We'll just take up a collection, and hand it over to Matt and Marie in a brown paper bag!"

"I don't have pots of money," Dru mumbled. "But there's twenty-five dollars in my account at the camp store. They can have that."

"Libby was teasing, Dru," Emily explained gently. "But it's nice of you to offer. I don't think twenty-five dollars is going to do it, though. Too bad none of us is really rich."

"Caro is," Danny said. Five heads swiveled in Caro's direction, and five pairs of eyes were riveted on the slender blond girl.

"Hey, that's right! Do you think maybe your folks would lend Matt and Marie some money to tide them over, Caro?" Lynda asked.

Caro stared down at her sandaled feet as though her brightly polished toenails were the most interesting things in the world. Finally, "No," she said.

"Why not? I bet they'd never miss it, if they're as rich as you're always saying they are," Libby added.

Caro looked up. "They're not. They're not rich at all," she sighed.

"But you said—" Danny began.

"I know what I said, but it wasn't true. I made it all up to impress everybody." She glanced at Emily. "Emily knows. I told her the other day. If Mother and Daddy really did have lots of money, I'd ask them, I honestly would. But they don't, so I can't."

After a long, stunned silence, Libby said, "Well, I'll be a monkey's uncle!"

"I wouldn't be a bit surprised," Caro retorted with a spark of her old feisty manner, and everyone laughed.

"You know," Emily said, "the more I think about it, the more it seems that money isn't really the answer. The Websters aren't starving, or anything. And they were all perfectly happy until Mr. Frick came along."

"We were *all* happy until Mr. Frick came along," Danny said.

"Love of money is the root of all evil, like my grandmother says," Libby added. She leaped to her feet and shinnied up the trunk of the tree, perching on a low, overhanging branch directly over the other girls' heads.

"I wouldn't go *that* far," Caro said with a frown.

"Emily's right," Lynda said. "The Websters don't love money. They love horses, Matt more than anybody. And I bet the only reason he agreed to sell his property to Mr. Frick is because he's afraid his family is missing out on the things other people have—like a new car every year, and Florida vacations, and a mink coat for Marie."

"But stuff like that isn't important," Emily said. "What's important is doing what you love, and when you look at it that way, the Websters have everything anybody could ever want."

"Sure they do. We all know that, and now Matt must, too. All he has to do is look at Pam and Marie's faces, and probably Chris and Warren are just as miserable as they are. So he's probably sorry he made a deal with Mr. Frick, but he can't get out of it. Mr. Frick won't *let* him get out of it."

"But what about the mortgage on the farm?" Danny asked.

Emily turned to her. "We don't know there *is* a mortgage, Danny."

"But in the book—"

"This isn't a story. This is real life," Caro reminded her. Then her shoulders slumped. "But what difference does it make? Unless Mr. Frick changes his mind, it's good-bye, Webster's, mortgage or no mortgage."

Everyone was silent, lost in glum thought. Suddenly Emily shouted, "Caro!"

Caro's head jerked up. "What? What's wrong? Is there a bug in my hair? I *hate* bugs!" She shook her ponytail frantically.

Emily giggled. "No, there's no bug. It's what you just said about Mr. Frick changing his mind!"

Hanging by her knees from the branch overhead, Libby said, "What about it? He's not going to change his mind. Why should he? The minute he owns Webster's, he can start bulldozing and making a fortune."

"Not if he thinks there's something wrong with the property, something that would make people not want to move here!" Emily's eyes were shining with excitement.

"But there *isn't* anything wrong with it," Dru said, puzzled. "Is there?"

Libby sat up on her branch. "Hey, I think I see

what Emily's driving at," she said. A mischievous grin spread over her freckled face. "There's nothing *really* wrong, but what if Mr. Frick *thought* there was?"

"That's a very clever idea, Emily," Caro said admiringly. Then she smirked. "I'm so glad I thought of it!"

Emily stared at her through narrowed eyes. Apparently Caro hadn't changed as much as Emily thought she had—she still had to come out on top, no matter what. Emily was about to straighten her out, when Caro's smirk turned into a real grin.

"Just kidding," she chirped. "But I had you going there for a minute, didn't I? Seriously, I think it's a terrific idea, and I bet it'll work, too."

"You mean, we tell Mr. Frick all sorts of bad things about Webster's so he won't buy it?" Penny asked. Her round blue eyes were worried. "That's not very honest."

"No, it's not," Emily admitted. "But look at it this way, Penny. By telling a few little white lies, we'll be doing a good deed for Matt, Marie, Pam, Chris, and Warren, not to mention the horses."

"Yes, Penny—you're a Girl Scout," Lynda pointed out. "Aren't Girl Scouts supposed to do good deeds every day, like Boy Scouts?"

"Well . . . yes . . ."

"If you help us save Webster's, that'll be enough good deeds to last the rest of the year," Libby said, and after a moment, Penny nodded.

"That's settled then," Lynda said. "Now everybody think real hard, and come up with things that will make Mr. Frick decide he doesn't want to buy Webster's after all."

"I have a great idea!" Emily cried eagerly. "Listen to this. . . ."

Chapter Five

The Fillies could hardly wait to put their plan into operation. But Mr. Frick didn't show up again that day.

"What if he doesn't come back at all?" Lynda asked worriedly as they piled into the camp van after supper. Rachel was driving the Fillies and Thoros into Winnepac to the movies. *The Black Stallion* was playing at the town's only theater, and though everyone had seen it at least twice, they all were eager to see it again.

"We could write him a letter," Dru suggested.

Emily shook her head. "That wouldn't work, even if we had his address, which we don't. We have to *show* him, not just tell him."

"He'll be back, I'm sure of it," Caro said. "He'll want to snoop around and gloat. I know his type!"

"Move over, Caro, you're hogging the whole seat," Nancy, a Thoro, said, squeezing in next to her. "What are all of you whispering about? Some big secret?"

Penny nodded. "A *very* big secret," she said solemnly.

Beth, another Thoro, leaned over from the seat behind them, asking, "What is it?"

"If we told you, it wouldn't be a secret anymore," Caro said sweetly.

"Eskimo Christian and Italian," Libby sang out.

Beth stared at her. "Huh?"

"Eskimo Christian and Italian no lies," Libby replied. "Is everybody on board? Come on, Rachel, let's go!"

Mr. Frick just has to show up, Emily thought as the van began jouncing over the dirt road toward Winnepac. *He* has *to!* But a little voice inside her head murmured, "What if he doesn't?"

The little voice was still nagging Emily the next morning as she went into the stable, but Libby's voice drowned it out almost at once.

"Foxy! Where's Foxy? He's not in his stall!"

Emily and several of the other campers went over to investigate and discovered that Foxy's stall was indeed empty.

"Maybe he's been horsenapped," suggested a wide-eyed Foal.

"I'm going to find Chris," Libby said. "He and Warren always bring the horses in from the pasture. He'll know where Foxy is."

"I'll come with you," Emily offered. They hurried off toward the door that led into the stable yard, where they met Chris coming in.

54

Before Libby could say a word, Chris held up one hand. "Don't get all excited," he said. "Foxy's okay. He's right over there by the fence. I didn't bring him inside because . . . well, see for yourself."

Libby and Emily both looked, and Foxy looked back at them from the other side of the yard, flicking his black-tipped ears back and forth and swishing his tail.

"He looks fine to me," Libby said. "Can I bring him in now?"

"Is something the matter with him?" Emily asked. Foxy looked fine to her, too.

Though he had been looking as sad as the rest of his family the last time Emily had seen him, now Chris grinned just a little. "Depends on how you look at it," he said in answer to Emily's question. "I guess I should have said *smell* for yourself!"

Libby and Emily moved closer to Foxy, sniffing the air.

"Phew!" Libby wrinkled her nose. "Skunk!"

"You got it," Chris said. "Seems like last night old Foxy met up with a skunk in the pasture somewhere, and the skunk wasn't too happy about it. He must've sprayed Foxy's legs or something—I didn't get close enough to check it out. I didn't want to stink up the whole stable, so I tied him up out here."

"Don't you *dare* bring that horse inside!" Caro shouted. "Skunk! How gross!"

"Oh, poor Foxy," Libby sighed. "I guess I better give him a bath. Emily, want to help me?"

"Sure," Emily said. "I can take care of Joker later. I'll go get a bucket and some soap."

"And I'll get the tomato juice," Chris said.

Libby and Emily stared at him. "Tomato juice?" they both echoed.

"Yeah. Tomato juice kills the smell of skunk. Don't ask me how, it just does. Be back in a flash." Chris trotted off toward the farmhouse as Emily and Libby looked at each other, amazed.

"Do you think he's putting us on?" Emily asked. "It sounds pretty weird to me!"

"It sounds weird, all right, but Chris usually knows what he's talking about," Libby said. "We might as well try it. You get that bucket, and some soap, and I'll pull out the hose. If the tomato juice *does* work, we'll have to wash it off Foxy afterward."

Emily ran back into the stable and ducked into the empty stall where various supplies were kept, the same stall where she'd found Dru the night Dru ran away from camp. She found a big bucket and a bar of yellow soap and grabbed a sponge from a shelf. Then she dropped the soap and the sponge into the bucket and went down to Joker's stall. The big palomino's head was sticking out over the door. He was obviously wondering where she was.

Emily rubbed between his ears and kissed his velvety nose. "Sorry, Joker! I have to help Libby for a while, but I'll take care of you as soon as I can. Here, have some toast." She fished the piece she'd saved for him at breakfast out of her jeans pocket and offered it to him on the palm of her hand. Joker nibbled it delicately. Emily stroked his neck, then hurried back to pick up her bucket and bring it out to the stable yard.

When she got there, Chris had returned with a big can of tomato juice. He took out the soap and the sponge and poured the red liquid into the bucket. "There you go," he said to Libby. "Have fun!" And he sprinted off.

Libby, holding her nose with one hand, dipped the sponge into the bucket with the other and began sponging Foxy's forelegs. Foxy didn't seem to mind at all. He just stood there, munching on the honeysuckle that grew along the fence, as though having a bath in tomato juice was something that happened every day.

"Does it sbell ady better?" Libby asked.

Emily, who was also holding her nose, replied, "I cad't tell."

"Well, let go of your dose ad fide out!"

Tentatively, Emily released one nostril, then the other, and sniffed. The nasty smell was fading. "Well, what do you know! It's working!" she cried.

Libby sniffed, too. "Thank goodness! Now let's use the soap. I'll go turn on the water."

She ran over to the spigot, and Emily directed the spray from the hose into the bucket, washing out what was left of the tomato juice. Soon the bucket was filled with bubbles from the yellow soap. Emily handed the soapy sponge to Libby, who began washing Foxy's front legs.

"Well, well! What have we here? A bubble bath?"

Both girls looked up to see Mr. Frick standing nearby. He was wearing a different suit today, and a neat little straw hat. His face was pink and friendly.

Emily and Libby looked at each other, communicating without words. Each knew what the other had in mind.

"It's because of the skunks," Libby said brightly. "There are so many skunks around here! They get scared when the horses—or people—come into their territory, and then they spray. One of them got Foxy last night."

"It happens all the time," Emily added. "You wouldn't *believe* how many skunks there are at Webster's! You have to be awfully careful wherever you go. Those skunks defend their territory like crazy."

"Yeah, and this isn't really a bubble bath," Libby said. "We've been kind of wondering about why the water comes out of the spigots all bubbly like this. I mean, the water here comes from an underground spring, so why should it have bubbles? Unless the spring has been polluted, or something."

"Gee, Libby, you don't think there's any truth to the rumor that there's an underground nuclear power plant up near Schenectady, do you?" Emily asked, glancing at Mr. Frick.

"Oh, I hope not!" Libby flung her arms around Foxy's neck. "I'd hate to think I was washing Foxy in radioactive water!"

Mr. Frick backed away a few steps, clutching his briefcase in both hands.

"Radioactive water?" he repeated.

59

"It's just a rumor," Emily hastened to assure him. "Nobody knows for sure. And if there was something like that going on, I'm positive Matt wouldn't keep the camp here. Unless he didn't know . . ."

"Skunks? Radioactive water?" Mr. Frick backed farther away. "Matt never said anything about—"

"Like Emily just said, maybe he doesn't know. And we don't, either, not for sure. But that's what we've heard."

"I see." Mr. Frick frowned and wiped the sweat off his forehead beneath the brim of his hat. "But that horse looks perfectly healthy."

"Oh, he is—for now." Libby patted Foxy's shoulder. "But who knows what will happen to him in a few years? Or even a few months?" She heaved a huge sigh.

"You never can tell," Emily said sorrowfully. "Webster's might turn into a disaster area. Nobody would want to come here at all."

"Please don't tell Matt what we just told you," Libby said. "We don't want him to be upset. He'll find out soon enough."

Mr. Frick's frown deepened. "A nuclear power plant somewhere near Schenectady, you say? That's odd—I live up that way myself, and I've never heard anything about it."

Emily smiled at him. "Oh, good! Then it's probably nothing but a rumor, and we don't have anything to worry about."

"But what about those bubbles?" Libby looked

down at the foamy bucket. "I suppose it *could* be some other kind of pollution. . . ."

Glancing at his watch, Mr. Frick said, "Well, time's a-wasting, and I have an appointment at ten-thirty, so I'd better be on my way. Nice meeting you both . . . by the way, what are your names? I'm Larry Frick."

"We know," Emily and Libby said together. Libby wiped her wet hand on her jeans and held it out. For a moment, it looked as if Mr. Frick was going to shake it. Then he looked at the bubbles and changed his mind. "I'm Libby Dexter, and this is Emily Jordan," Libby said.

Mr. Frick nodded. "Libby and Emily. I'll remember that. Be seeing you." He tipped his hat and went out of the stable yard, watching his step very carefully.

The girls waited until he disappeared around the corner of the stable. When they were sure he couldn't hear them, they threw their arms around each other and jumped up and down.

"Did you see his face when we told him about the skunks?" Emily said between giggles.

"Did I ever! And then when we just happened to mention the radioactive water . . ."

"That really got to him, all right! Boy, were we ever lucky that he turned up when he did. I couldn't figure out how we were going to bring up the nuclear power plant. It was a stroke of genius when you came up with the bubble theory!"

"Maybe not genius exactly," Libby said modestly.

"I'll settle for brilliant. And you followed through beautifully. I bet Mr. Frick is having second thoughts already about buying this place."

"By the time we're through with him, he'll be having third, fourth, and fifth thoughts!" Emily chortled.

Just then Pam stepped out into the stable yard. "Libby, Emily, aren't you finished deodorizing that horse yet?" she called. "Riding classes begin in less than half an hour."

"We're done," Libby shouted, and Pam went back inside. Libby untied Foxy from the fence and led him into the stable while Emily emptied the soapy water and returned the bucket, sponge, and soap to the storage room. Then she headed for Joker's stall, whistling a little tune under her breath. She didn't see Matt until she almost ran right into him.

"Whoa, where's the fire?" he said, smiling.

Emily beamed at him. "I was helping Libby with Foxy. He had a close encounter with a skunk last night, and we had to give him a bath, so I'm in a rush to do my stable chores and groom Joker."

"Yes, I heard about the skunk from Chris . . . and from Larry Frick. He told me he had a very interesting conversation with you and Libby."

"Oh, yes. It was *very* interesting." Emily hesitated. "Uh . . . did Mr. Frick tell you what else we talked about, besides the skunk, that is?"

"Not really. He was in a big hurry . . . said he didn't want to be late for an appointment."

"Good!" Emily said, then added quickly, "I'm kind of in a big hurry, too, so if you'll excuse me. . . ." She sidestepped around him and ducked into Joker's stall.

"Since it's almost time for class, why don't you forget about cleaning out the stall for now and concentrate on Joker?" Matt suggested. "You can do your housekeeping later."

Emily laughed. "Thanks, Matt. I like *horsekeeping* a lot better than housekeeping."

Matt shook his head in mock dismay. "Oh, Emily, that was really bad!" But he was smiling again as he strode off, and that made Emily feel good. If the Fillies' plan worked, she was sure Matt would be smiling all the time, and so would the rest of the Websters.

It didn't take long for Emily to brush and polish Joker's golden coat to a glossy sheen. But getting the burrs out of his flowing white tail was another matter entirely. She worked very carefully and gently, using her fingers and a metal comb, until she had removed every single one. Then she saddled and bridled him, stuck her riding hat on her head, and trotted him out of the stable just in time to join the other campers on their way to the riding rings.

"Libby told me about what you said to Mr. Frick," Penny said, coming up next to her on her horse, Pepper. "She said it really made an impression on him."

"I think it did. But that's just the beginning," Emily said. "Wait till Danny does her number on

63

him. If that doesn't drive him away from Webster's for good, I'll eat my hat."

Penny giggled. "Then I hope it does the trick, or else you're going to have an awful case of indigestion!"

Chapter Six

An opportunity to put step two of their plan into effect arose the very next afternoon. Though the Fillies were on dish detail after supper that evening, Emily, Danny, and Lynda had volunteered to pick blueberries for dessert, and Marie had promised to bake blueberry muffins for tomorrow's breakfast if there were enough left over.

"I wonder where Mr. Frick's been keeping himself lately," Lynda said as the girls finished filling their baskets.

"I sure hope he hasn't been trying to find out about that secret nuclear power plant," Emily said. "If I'd known he lived near Schenectady, I would have chosen another city."

They started back toward camp, skirting the vegetable garden where the Thoros were still picking lettuce, tomatoes, cucumbers, green beans . . . and of course, squash. Suddenly Danny put a hand on Emily's arm.

"Look over there! Isn't that Mr. Frick standing under that tree?"

Emily and Lynda looked, and Emily nodded. "That's him, all right. Are you ready to do your thing, Danny?"

"As ready as I'll ever be, I guess," Danny said nervously. "But you both have to back me up, okay?"

"Absolutely!" Lynda said. They changed course, cutting across the grass in Mr. Frick's direction.

He was so absorbed in studying some papers he was holding that he didn't notice their approach. Today he was wearing a short-sleeved shirt and a bright red bow tie, and his suit jacket was neatly folded over one arm.

"Hi, Mr. Frick! Hot enough for you?" Emily said brightly when she, Danny, and Lynda were within a few feet of him.

Mr. Frick glanced up, startled. "Oh, hello, girls." He looked at Emily. "Emily Jordan, right?" When Emily nodded, he smiled broadly. "I never forget a name, or a face. And who are these two young ladies?"

Emily introduced Lynda and Danny, and Mr. Frick nodded pleasantly as he rolled up his papers and put them into a cardboard tube that was tucked under his arm.

"Well, well!" he said. "Blueberry picking, I see. And nice, big, fat ones, too. Mind if I taste a few?"

"Be my guest," Lynda said, offering him her basket. He scooped up a handful and popped them into his mouth one by one.

"Mmmm—delicious! Don't know why it is, but everything Matt and Marie grow tastes better than the same thing anywhere else. Maybe it's because they don't use any pesticides. All natural, organic gardening—that's the ticket."

Lynda sighed. "Yes. It's too bad it can't stay that way."

"It can't? Why not?" Mr. Frick asked.

"Because—" Lynda began, but she was interrupted by a faint moan from Danny.

"What is it, Danny?" Emily asked.

"Ooohhh . . ." Danny carefully set down her basket, then clutched her head with both hands, weaving a little on her feet. "My head . . . I feel so dizzy. . . ."

"Here—sit down." Lynda led Danny to the base of the tree, and Danny leaned against it, sliding down to a sitting position.

"What's wrong with her?" Mr. Frick peered at her anxiously. "Too much sun?"

Lynda shook her head. "I wish that was all it was. No, I'm afraid it's The Fever."

"Ooooooohh," Danny moaned again.

Mr. Frick looked from Lynda to Emily. "What fever? What are you talking about?"

"I guess you've heard of Rocky Mountain Spotted Fever," Emily said, reaching down to pat Danny's dark head.

"Of course I have. Don't tell me that's what she's got?" Mr. Frick gasped.

"No—it's worse. Much worse," Lynda said sadly. "It's the Adirondack Blueberry Fever!"

Mr. Frick's pink face grew suddenly pale. "Do you get it from *eating* blueberries?"

"Oh, no," Emily assured him, and he visibly relaxed. "No," she went on, "you get it from the bite of a tiny little insect that lives on blueberry bushes. One of them must have bitten Danny."

"That's what I was about to say before," Lynda put in. "The Websters are going to have to start spraying their berry bushes to get rid of the blueberry bugs. But it might take *years* to wipe them out, and in the meantime . . ."

"In the meantime, people who are very susceptible, like Danny, will keep coming down with The Fever," Emily said. "It's not fatal or anything, and the symptoms usually go away in a few hours, but they can keep coming back. There's no cure for it, as far as I know, but I'm sure medical science will come up with something one of these days."

Danny grabbed Emily's hand. "Please don't tell Matt and Marie! I'm sure I'll be fine in a little while. I don't want to go to the hospital, and miss the horse show on Sunday!"

"We won't tell," Emily soothed. "And you won't either, will you, Mr. Frick? They'd feel terrible if they knew Danny got sick because of their blueberry bugs."

"Not only that, but if word got out, all the campers' parents would take them away. Nobody would want to come within a mile of Webster's if they knew," Lynda added.

"Now just a minute!" Mr. Frick was starting to look very skeptical. "I've never heard of Adirondack Blueberry Fever in all the years I've been living in this area."

"I'm not surprised," Danny said in a weak little voice. "It's not the sort of thing people talk about much. And that's not the real name of it, either. That's just what we call it."

"And in spite of all this, you're taking all these blueberries back to the camp?"

"Oh, yes. It's all right. The insects never come near the berries, just the leaves," Lynda said. "And not just blueberry leaves, either. Matt will probably have to spray the entire property to get rid of them all."

Mr. Frick glanced up at the lush green leaves under which he was standing and hastily moved out into the late afternoon sunshine. Taking a ballpoint pen out of a little plastic liner in his shirt pocket, he said, "This bears looking into. What is the actual name of this disease?" Now he took a notebook out of his hip pocket, opened it, and waited for a reply.

Uh-oh, Emily thought. They hadn't expected anything like this. "Gosh, I'm not exactly sure," she hedged. "I think it starts with *t-z-r,* but I'm not positive."

"No, you're wrong, Emily," Lynda said firmly. "I saw it in a magazine once, and it starts with *t-c-h.*"

70

"You're both wrong," Danny said. "It doesn't start with *t* at all. It's *c-h-r-z* . . . something." As an afterthought, she threw in a faint moan.

"Oh, my goodness! It's so complicated we can't even *pronounce* it, much less spell it," Emily said.

Mr. Frick snapped his notebook closed and shoved the pen back into his pocket. "I see. Well, I'll just have to do some research on my own. And now I must be on my way. Unless you'd like me to help you to the farmhouse?" he said to Danny. "Though I must say you're looking much better."

"I *am* much better, thanks." Danny gave him a wan smile.

"Would you like to take some blueberries with you?" Lynda suggested brightly. "We have more than enough."

But Mr. Frick was already on his way. "No!" he called back over his shoulder. "Er . . . no, thank you. The ones I ate before don't seem to be sitting very well for some reason."

He hurried along without another backward glance as the girls watched, restraining their laughter with great difficulty. Suddenly Mr. Frick froze, staring at something in the bushes nearby. Emily, Lynda, and Danny strained to see what it was, and couldn't have been more delighted when a small black creature with a white stripe down its back ambled out.

"The skunk! Foxy's skunk!" Emily whispered. "What perfect timing!"

71

The skunk paused when it saw Mr. Frick, and Mr. Frick didn't move a muscle.

"Do you think it's going to . . . ?" Danny asked.

"Not unless Mr. Frick does something to scare it," Lynda replied.

Emily stifled a snort of laughter. "If he does, I hope Marie has lots more tomato juice on hand!"

Mr. Frick and the skunk stared at each other for what seemed a very long time. Then the skunk turned around and went back the way it had come. Mr. Frick waited a moment longer to make sure it was really gone. Convinced that the coast was clear, he took off at a jog-trot and didn't stop until he reached a shiny red car by the side of the dirt road. He leaped in, slammed the door, gunned the engine, and drove off in a cloud of dust.

Whooping with laughter, Emily and Lynda sank down beside Danny.

"Ooooohh," Danny groaned, but from mirth this time. "That was too good to be true!"

Lynda gasped between giggles. "He must think Webster's is *crawling* with skunks and evil insects!"

"And I bet he'll never eat another blueberry as long as he lives," Emily cried. "You were fantastic, Danny. I never knew you were such a good actress."

Danny grinned. "Neither did I! Actually, the credit should go to Caro."

"Caro?" Lynda echoed. "She wasn't even here."

"I know, but I remembered how she used to fake those terrible headaches when she wanted to get out of doing her chores, and I just did the same thing."

That made them laugh even harder. When at last they dried their eyes and pulled themselves together, they all got to their feet and picked up their baskets. Lynda said, "If we don't make tracks, there won't be time for Marie to see if there'll be enough left over for muffins."

They started off for the farmhouse, waving at the last of the Thoros who had finished garden detail and were straggling ahead of them with the vegetables for supper. After a while, Danny said, "You're awfully quiet, Emily."

Emily, who had been lost in thought, raised her head. "Yeah, I know."

"Something wrong?" Lynda asked.

"Not wrong, exactly . . ." It was difficult for Emily to put into words what had been going through her mind, because her thoughts were all jumbled up.

"I know. She's coming down with an attack of Adirondack Blueberry Fever!" Danny said.

Emily gave her a poke. "Bite your tongue!" She tossed a few berries into her mouth from her basket, but they didn't taste quite as good as they had earlier. "I was just thinking. . . . Mr. Frick didn't seem completely convinced of what we were telling him. I'm not sure he believed that Danny was really sick."

Danny frowned. "But you just said I was a good actress."

"You were—you are. That's not the point."

"Then what *is* the point?" Lynda asked.

After a pause, Emily said, "I don't think Mr. Frick is as dumb as we think he is. From everything we know about him—and I admit that isn't much—he's a very successful businessman. You don't get to be a success if you're dumb. I just don't think he's going to take our word for it that Webster's is infested with blueberry bugs. I bet he's going to check it out, ask questions, maybe even try to find Adirondack Blueberry Fever in a medical encyclopedia or something."

"But we told him that's not the real name of the disease," Danny said. "He doesn't even know if it begins with a *t* or a *c*!"

Emily shrugged. "I know. But if he starts asking questions about the secret nuclear power plant and the Blueberry Fever, and he doesn't come up with anything, he's going to start wondering if somebody's been putting him on. He might even talk to Matt about it."

"Well, we just have to hope that he doesn't!" Danny ran ahead, opening the back door of the farmhouse. "Marie, we have enough blueberries for an army! Muffins for breakfast, okay?"

Chapter Seven

It wasn't until the following day that Emily realized she had never finished the letter she'd started to Judy on Monday. There just hadn't been time, and she had been too concerned about the future of Webster's even to think about anything else. So during rest period, she took out her stationery and picked up where she'd left off, telling Judy all about Mr. Frick and the Fillies' fears about what he was going to do if he bought Matt's property. She also explained their plan to make him change his mind, describing in detail the incident with Foxy, the skunk, and the bubble bath, and Danny's performance as a victim of Adirondack Blueberry Fever—she knew Judy would get a kick out of that!

Then she scribbled a note to her parents, feeling a little guilty because she never wrote as much to them as she did to Judy. Emily didn't tell them about Mr. Frick, though. She had a sneaking suspicion they might think she was overreacting and letting her imagination run away with her.

Caro had been writing letters, too, and Emily had a pretty good idea that one of them was to Eric. Caro had been rather quiet lately, and Emily thought she knew why. So far, Eric hadn't written to her, and Emily was sure she must be feeling kind of blue. It was funny, when she thought about it—Emily had been convinced that Caro would forget all about Eric after he was gone, and that Eric would be the one whose heart would get broken, or at least bruised. Only it was the other way around, and Emily couldn't help feeling sorry for Caro.

"Are you going up to the mailbox, Emily?" Caro asked as Emily finished addressing and stamping her letters.

"Yeah. What about you?" Emily slipped her bare feet into her rubber thong sandals and slung a towel over her shoulder. She planned on going directly down to the dock for water sports after she visited the mailbox, and she was already wearing her yellow-and-blue tank suit.

"Me, too." Caro fell into step beside her, and the two of them left the cabin, telling Penny and Dru, the only Fillies who were there, that they'd see them in a few minutes. Penny and Dru were concentrating on a game of War, and didn't seem to notice.

Neither Caro nor Emily spoke for a while. It was Caro who finally broke the silence. "Emily, you told me that Eric didn't have a girlfriend, right?"

"That's right. Unless you count Rita Rodriguez."
Caro frowned. "Who's Rita Rodriguez?"
Emily wished she hadn't mentioned Rita. She'd

been thinking about Mr. Frick, and the name had just slipped out. Now she said, "She's a girl who works at the supermarket where Eric has a summer job. He took her to the movies once or twice. But she's not really a girlfriend."

Caro heaved a heavy sigh. "Maybe she is now. Maybe he's so busy with Rita Rodriguez that he hasn't had time to write to me—not so much as a postcard!"

"Hey, Caro, you have to understand something about my brother," Emily said. "He is without doubt the world's *worst* letter writer! I've been here for almost five weeks, and he's never written to me once."

"Yes, but you're his *sister*," Caro pointed out. "And he promised to write to me, and I've written *four* letters to him!"

"Four letters?" Emily was impressed. "Four letters in four days? Wow!"

"I just wrote him another one," Caro confessed miserably. "I thought he really liked me, but I guess he doesn't. I think I'll just tear this letter up!"

"Don't do that, Caro," Emily said. "Think of how much stamps cost! It would be like throwing money away."

Caro sighed again. "I could always soak off the stamp."

"Oh, rats!" Emily exclaimed. "There goes the mail truck. We're too late for him to pick up our letters anyway."

"I think I'll soak off the stamp," Caro mumbled.

Emily ran ahead and opened the mailbox in front of the farmhouse. It was filled with letters, postcards, and junk mail, and she pulled everything out. An envelope dropped to the ground. She bent down to pick it up, but Caro got there first. She was about to hand it over to Emily, when she saw the name on it.

"It's for me!" she cried. "And the postmark is Hamilton, Pennsylvania!"

Emily looked at it. "That's Eric's handwriting, all right. Are you sure you want to soak off that stamp?"

Caro's pretty face was glowing as she shoved her letters into the mailbox along with Emily's. "No way! He wrote to me! He actually *wrote* to me!"

Emily put her two letters in with Caro's. "The mailman will pick them up tomorrow." She riffled through the mail she was holding and saw a letter from Judy, one from her parents, and another from her grandmother. She took her own mail and said, "I'll take the rest into the camp store. Wait for me, okay?"

But Caro didn't answer. She had ripped open Eric's letter and was reading it happily. Emily ran up onto the porch of the farmhouse, dropped the rest of the mail onto the counter of the camp store, and hurried back to find Caro smiling.

"He's sorry he couldn't write before, but there was a flood in the basement of the supermarket," she sighed. Her big, beautiful eyes were starry as she added, "A water main broke, and hundreds of pounds of flour and cereal were completely *ruined*!

And he's been working overtime to clean up the mess. His sneakers have been soaked for *days*, and he's afraid he's going to get athlete's foot!"

"Gee, that's really romantic," Emily said solemnly, trying to keep a straight face.

Caro didn't seem to hear. "And listen to this— 'This girl I used to work with, Rita Rodriguez, quit yesterday, because she didn't like wading around in all that water. So that means that I'm going to be a cashier, not just a bagger, and I'll be making more money, so maybe I can come visit you over Thanksgiving, if your folks don't mind.'" Caro beamed at Emily. "So much for Rita Rodriguez!"

Though Emily wasn't too happy at the thought of Eric not being with the rest of the family for the holiday, she smiled at Caro anyway. "That's nice. But if Eric *does* go to your house for Thanksgiving, be sure to tell your mother that he only likes white meat, and he can't *stand* creamed onions."

"Neither can I," Caro said happily. "I knew we were made for each other!"

After water sports, the Fillies put on their riding clothes again and hurried to the stables to saddle their horses. Pam had told them that they were going to follow a new trail that Warren and Chris had been clearing through the woods, and everybody was looking forward to it.

As Emily rode out into the stable yard between Caro and Dru, she was surprised to see Matt coming through the gate with Mr. Frick at his side. Instead of his usual business suit, Mr. Frick was wearing riding breeches, shiny new boots, and a velvet-covered hard hat that looked too big for his head.

"What's *he* doing here?" Caro asked out of the side of her mouth. "And why on earth is he dressed like that?"

"You don't suppose he's going to come with us, do you?" Dru whispered.

"It sure looks like it," Emily said. "Sssh. Here they come."

"Hello, girls," Matt said. "You're going to have a couple of extra riders with your group this afternoon. Hope you don't mind. Caroline Lescaux, Dru Carpenter, this is my friend and business associate, Larry Frick. Larry, I believe you and Emily have already met."

Mr. Frick nodded, giving Emily a wary look. "We have indeed. Twice. How's your friend, Emily? Is she completely recovered from her attack?"

"Attack? What attack?" Matt asked, puzzled.

"Oh, she's just fine," Emily said quickly. The other Fillies were riding into the stable yard, Danny in the lead on Misty, her black mare. "See for yourself. Here she comes now."

Danny smiled and waved, and so did Libby. Then Pam rode out on her rangy bay gelding, Firefly. "Warren's bringing out Mr. Frick's horse," she told her father.

"Er . . . I hope it's a gentle animal," Mr. Frick said nervously. "I'm not a very experienced rider, you know."

"Gideon's as gentle as a lamb," Pam assured him. "You won't have any trouble with him, I promise."

Mr. Frick didn't look convinced. "I certainly hope you're right," he said, eyeing the stocky piebald Warren was leading over to the mounting block.

As Warren gave him a leg up into the saddle and adjusted the stirrup leathers, he said, "I saddled Pogo for you, Dad, but I didn't tack up Queenie yet because I didn't know if Mom was coming."

Matt shook his head. "Afraid not, son. She's not feeling up to it today. Besides, she's expecting an important phone call."

"I'll bet!" Libby muttered. She and Emily walked their horses away from the group so Matt and Mr. Frick couldn't hear. "She probably can't stand the thought of seeing that man riding one of Webster's horses, knowing that pretty soon they'll be *his* horses."

"Not if we can help it," Emily said. "And I hope we can. But our plan doesn't seem to be working very well. Mr. Frick wouldn't be riding with us if he'd changed his mind about buying the camp."

Libby sighed. "I know, darn it!"

A few minutes later, Matt swung effortlessly into Pogo's saddle. Emily thought he looked wonderful on horseback, as if that were where he belonged. And he *did* belong there. Matt Webster had ridden champion jumpers on the show circuit for many years before he had retired and begun a second career with the farm and camp. Pogo, his huge chestnut gelding, had won many ribbons and trophies before he, too, had retired from competition.

Mr. Frick, on the other hand, obviously belonged anywhere but on a horse. If he were a camper at Webster's Emily was sure he'd be in the beginners' riding class. His shiny new boots were shoved all the way through the stirrups, and though Warren tried several times to show him how to hold the reins, he couldn't seem to catch on. When the horses started to move out behind Pam, Mr. Frick grabbed hold of the saddle and hung on for dear life.

"He rides worse than I did when I first came here," Dru giggled.

Emily looked over her shoulder at Mr. Frick and Matt, who were bringing up the rear. "He sure does. *Much* worse."

"Maybe he'll fall off," Penny suggested hopefully. Then she added, "Not that I'd want him to be hurt or anything, but it would serve him right."

"Nobody could fall off Gideon," Libby said.

"That's what everybody said about Donna," Dru reminded her, patting her mare's shoulder. "But *I* fell off."

The trail ride proceeded without incident, however. After a while, Emily almost forgot about Mr. Frick. The new trail wound through a section of the woods where she had never been before, and she enjoyed taking a different route for a change. The air was cool and pleasant under the trees. Looking up, Emily could see patches of bright blue sky between the branches. She also saw, to her surprise, that some of the leaves were beginning to turn red and gold. She remembered watching the Canada geese flying south, another indication that autumn was on its way. But she didn't want to think about that. She'd much rather pretend that the summer would go on forever.

"Let's sing something," Caro suggested as they rode along.

"How about 'Camptown Races'?" Lynda said, and all the Fillies began to sing:

"The Camptown ladies sing this song,
Doo-dah, doo-dah,
Camptown racetrack five miles long,
Oh, doo-dah day!
Gonna run all night, gonna run all day,
I bet my money on a bob-tailed nag,
Somebody bet on the bay.
The long-tailed filly and the big black hoss,
Doo-dah, doo-dah,
They fly the track and they both cut across,
Oh, doo-dah day. . . ."

"Who's the long-tailed filly?" Lynda called, laughing.

Caro held up her blond ponytail and waved it. "Why, me, of course!"

"The blind hoss stick in a big mud hole,
Doo-dah, doo-dah,
Can't touch bottom with a ten-foot pole,

84

Oh, doo-dah day!
Gonna run all night, gonna run all day,
I bet my money on a bob-tailed nag,
Somebody bet on the bay. . . ."

When they had finished all the verses of the song, Pam shouted, "Heads up, Fillies and Mr. Frick. Chris and Warren did a great job of clearing the underbrush, but there are still some low-hanging limbs they haven't gotten around to trimming yet. Keep your eyes open and look where you're going so you don't get swept out of the saddle."

All the Fillies did as they were told, but Emily, who had fallen back near the end of the line, noticed that Mr. Frick seemingly hadn't heard Pam. Because the horses were in single file, he kept turning around to talk to Matt, who was directly behind him. Emily saw a big, low branch ahead. Everyone was ducking as their horses passed under it, and Emily did, too. By this time, Mr. Frick and Matt were some distance behind the other horses.

Suddenly Emily heard Matt call out, "Larry! Slow him down! Pull back on the reins. . . . Larry, *look out!*"

She turned around just as Gideon approached the limb at a brisk trot, apparently in a hurry to catch up with the rest. Now Mr. Frick saw the overhanging branch, but it was too late. The branch only grazed the top of his hard hat, but Mr. Frick, who had let go of the reins, lost his balance and toppled to the ground in spite of Matt's attempt to grab his arm.

85

He landed with a loud "*Oof!*" and Gideon trotted a few paces more, then stopped right behind Lynda's gray gelding, Dan.

"Pam—everybody—stop!" Emily yelled as Matt leaped out of the saddle and knelt beside Mr. Frick.

The Fillies pulled their horses to a halt, and they all craned their necks to see what was going on. In the silence, Penny's voice could be clearly heard. "Oh, gee! He *did* fall off!"

"Larry, are you okay?" Matt asked anxiously. "Can you move?"

Mr. Frick slowly sat up, rubbing his neck, then each arm and leg. Satisfied that he was all in one piece, Matt stood up and stretched out a hand, pulling him to his feet.

"Gentle as a lamb, eh?" Mr. Frick said grimly. He brushed dirt and leaves from his clothing and settled his hat more firmly on his head. "Webster, that horse is a menace! This is the last straw! I've tried to overlook the other hazards of this operation, but now I'm convinced that I've been making a big mistake. I think it's time we had a serious talk, and the sooner the better!"

Emily's heart leaped. It seemed that their plan had worked after all, though Gideon hadn't been a part of it. She decided to give the piebald a special treat as soon as they got back to Webster's.

Now Matt was saying, "I don't know what you mean about 'the other hazards,' but I'm certainly willing to discuss things. We can go back to camp right now if you like. Do you feel up to getting back on Gideon?"

Mr. Frick hesitated. Then, aware of all the Fillies' eyes on him, he marched over to Gideon, seized the reins, and said, "No four-legged brute is going to get the best of me!" Refusing Matt's offer of help, he managed after a few unsuccessful attempts to clamber up into the saddle. "Let's go," he said, jerking Gideon's head around in the direction they had come.

"Pam, Mr. Frick and I are returning to camp," Matt said loudly so his daughter could hear. "You finish your trail ride. There's nothing to worry about. Mr. Frick hasn't been hurt, just shaken up a little."

He mounted Pogo, and he and his companion began to retrace their steps. Emily watched them until they were out of sight, then urged Joker forward to rejoin the others.

"He's changed his mind, all right," Libby said happily. "There's no way in the world he's going to buy Webster's after this!"

Emily grinned. "Better believe it! He can build his vacation homes and his shopping center somewhere else, somewhere far away."

Penny murmured, "I'm awfully glad he wasn't hurt. But I'm even gladder that he's not going to destroy Webster's."

"I think it's time for another song," Lynda said. "Let's sing 'The Old Gray Mare.'" She began to sing, and everyone joined in:

"The old gray mare, she ain't what she used to be,
Ain't what she used to be,
Ain't what she used to be.
The old gray mare, she ain't what she used to be—"

"And neither is Mr. Frick!" Libby giggled.

Chapter Eight

The Fillies returned to camp about an hour later. They cooled down their horses, unsaddled them, and saw that they had plenty of fresh hay and oats before they went back to the bunkhouse to wash up for supper. Pam had taken off for the farmhouse as soon as she had finished caring for Firefly, telling them that she would meet them in the dining room.

"I can't wait to find out what happened," Libby said to Emily as they changed into clean jeans and sweatshirts.

"Do you think Pam will tell us?" Emily asked as she tied the laces of her sneakers. "She doesn't know *we* know what's been going on."

"If she doesn't, we'll just have to ask her," Caro said, braiding her hair and tying the end with a bright pink ribbon. "There! I'm ready. And I'm absolutely starving! Anybody take a look at the menu for tonight?"

"Some kind of casserole, I think," Dru told her. "And lots of salad."

"Squashies for dessert," Penny added. "You know, squashies aren't all that bad."

"Yeah. They don't taste like squash at all," Lynda agreed. "I wonder where Mr. Frick is eating tonight."

"I don't care where he's eating, as long as it's not with us," Emily said. "I hope we've seen the last of Mr. Frick."

Just then, to the Fillies' surprise, Pam came into the cabin, slamming the screen door behind her. For the first time in days, she looked really happy. "Hi, gang," she said cheerfully. She pulled off her riding boots and started taking off her jeans.

"Hey, Pam, what's happening?" Libby asked eagerly.

Pam grinned. "Great news! Everything's going to be okay!"

"Terrific!" Emily cried. "Tell us about it."

Pam put on a clean pair of jeans and pulled on a T-shirt as she said, "Well, Mom's sister called."

"Marie's sister? Her twin sister?" Emily asked, wondering what that had to do with anything. Marie had told her how much she had missed her twin the first time the sisters went to different camps for the summer. She had been trying to cheer Emily up when Emily had been feeling awfully lonely for Judy her first day at camp. Marie had assured Emily that she'd soon feel much better, and indeed Emily had.

"That's right . . . Aunt Marjorie," Pam said. "She's my favorite aunt . . . Chris and Warren's favorite, too. I guess you've all been wondering why

Mom and Dad and the rest of us have been kind of depressed lately. We've all been terribly worried about Aunt Marjorie. She was in a bad car accident, and it looked like she wasn't going to live. She and Uncle Bill just moved to Oregon, and Mom wanted to go to her, but she couldn't get away because of all her responsibilities here. And today, while we were on the trail ride, Uncle Bill called to say that Aunt Marjorie is much better. She's going to be all right!"

"That's wonderful, Pam," Libby said. "I'm really glad your aunt's okay."

"That's what's been upsetting you?" Penny said. "Then it wasn't . . ."

"We thought it was . . ." Dru's voice trailed off.

Pam looked around at the Fillies' faces. "You thought it was what?"

"Hasn't anything else been bothering you?" Emily asked. "Something . . . well, something closer to home?"

Pam finished changing her clothes, tucking a fresh plaid shirt into her clean jeans. She looked very puzzled. "No, there's nothing else. As a matter of fact, things could hardly be better. And now that Aunt Marjorie's out of danger, everything's just about perfect."

"What about Mr. Frick?" Lynda said.

"Mr. Frick? Oh, you mean his fall this afternoon? He wasn't hurt at all. Nothing to worry about there."

"And Matt's not going to sell him his land?"

Emily said eagerly. "Mr. Frick's decided he doesn't want it after all?"

"Of course Dad's not going to sell. I told you that. Didn't you believe me?"

"Oh, we believed you," Dru said. "But he's been hanging around so much lately that we thought maybe he was trying to talk Matt into it. . . ."

"And that Matt had changed his mind, and you knew about it, but you didn't want to talk about it, and that's why all of you were so unhappy," Penny finished for her.

Pam laughed. "Boy, were you ever wrong! It's nothing like that at all. In fact, it's Dad who's been trying to talk Mr. Frick into something! I didn't want to tell you about it because it wasn't definite, but I guess there's no harm in telling you now." She beamed at all of them. "Remember I told you that we were kind of short of cash?" The girls nodded. "Well, we won't be anymore. The reason Mr. Frick has been here a lot is because he's been checking out the camp to see if it's a good business proposition. He's just about decided to become Dad's partner, and invest a lot of money in Webster's! Isn't that great? He wants to build a swimming pool, and put in a tennis court, and add some more cabins so we can have more campers next year. We're all very excited about it."

There was a long silence, during which Emily felt as if her stomach was slowly sinking down to her toes. When she was able to speak, her voice came out in a funny little croak. "That's great, all right."

"Oh, wow!" Lynda whispered. "I don't *believe* this!"

"The nuclear power plant," Libby mumbled.

"Skunks," Emily moaned.

"Adirondack Blueberry Fever," Danny gasped.

Pam stared at them. "What's the matter with you guys, anyway? I thought you'd be happy that Webster's is going to be bigger and better than ever before, but you sure don't *look* happy."

"We're happy. We're *very* happy," Caro said miserably. "We couldn't be happier."

"You certainly have a funny way of showing it!" Pam said. "Look, I have to run. Dad and Mr. Frick were going to decide when to sign the papers this afternoon after the trail ride. I'm going up to the house to find out if it's all settled. See you at supper, okay? Don't be late—we're going to have a lot to celebrate!"

As soon as she had left the bunkhouse, the Fillies let out a collective groan.

Libby looked at Emily. "Are you thinking what I'm thinking?"

"Probably," Emily sighed. "We blew it!"

"Did we ever!" Caro flopped down on her bunk. "We wanted to save Webster's, but it looks like we've ruined everything!"

"I think I'm going to be sick," Dru said in a small voice.

"Me, too," Penny added.

"After what we've done to Mr. Frick, it'll be a miracle if he wants to be Matt's business partner now," Lynda said dolefully.

"Nothing like this ever happened in any of the books I've read," Danny sighed.

"Well, at least we didn't make him fall off his horse," Emily said, trying to sound cheerful. "He did that all by himself."

"Yeah, but you heard what he said," Libby told her. "He said it was the last straw—the straw that broke the camel's back, like my grandmother says."

Another silence, even longer this time. It was broken by the distant clang of the dinner bell, calling all the campers to supper.

Dru mumbled, "I'm not hungry at all."

"Nobody's hungry," Lynda said, plodding toward the door. "But we have to show up for supper."

Emily followed her, but her feet felt as though they were weighted with lead. "I don't think there's going to be much of a celebration tonight. I have a very strong feeling that we're in big trouble, and it's all my fault."

"It's not *all* your fault, Emily," Caro said. "If things were the way we thought they were, it would be different. . . ."

"But they're not." Emily looked up at the clear blue sky. Barn swallows were soaring and dipping overhead, and locusts were singing an end-of-summer song. Chris would have taken the horses to their nighttime pasture by now. The mares and foals would be settling down for the evening, and the sheep and lambs would, too. And where was Mr.

Frick? Probably heading for Schenectady in his shiny red car, after telling Matt that never in a million years would he become Matt's partner in a camp that was so full of dangers and hazards.

Penny was right, Emily thought. Lies, even little white ones, could never lead to anything good. And no matter what Caro said, it really *was* all her fault.

The Fillies only picked at the good supper that Marie had prepared. The chicken and vegetable casserole tasted like sawdust to Emily, the salad had no flavor at all, and even the squashies tasted like cardboard. Pam didn't have much to say. When Lynda tentatively asked her what had happened with Matt and Mr. Frick, she just shrugged and said that nothing had been decided yet.

As the Fillies were clearing the tables after dinner, Matt came over to Emily and said, "I think we have to have a little talk."

"Just you and me?" Emily asked nervously.

"No," Matt said. "You, and Libby, Lynda, and Danny. When you're finished with dish detail, please come into the living room—there's not room for all of us in my office."

Emily swallowed. "Yes, sir. We'll be there in a few minutes." As Matt left the room, Emily, Libby, Danny, and Lynda looked at each other unhappily.

"Somehow I don't think he wants to give us the Camper of the Week award," Libby said.

Caro hurried over to them, a tray of dirty dishes in her hands. "What did Matt say?" she asked.

96

"He wants to see Libby, Lynda, Danny, and me right away," Emily told her.

"And that probably means that Mr. Frick has told him everything, and that he's not going to be Matt's partner," Danny sighed.

"We'll come with you," Penny said promptly. "After all, we all agreed to the plan."

Dru nodded. "Yes, we're all to blame. It's not fair for the four of you to be punished, or yelled at, or maybe even kicked out of camp."

Caro glared at her. "Dru! What a thing to say! Matt's not going to do anything like that. But I agree that we all ought to face him together. All for one, and one for all, remember?"

Emily was grateful for the others' support, but she shook her head and piled some plates and glasses on her tray. "No, Matt wants to see just the four of us because we were the ones who actually lied to Mr. Frick. We'll tell you about it . . . afterward."

Silently the girls finished clearing the tables and put the dirty dishes in the two big dishwashers in the kitchen. Marie smiled warmly at them, and Emily remembered to tell her how glad they were that her sister was out of danger.

"Thank you, Emily," Marie said. "It's a tremendous load off our minds, as you can imagine."

"Uh . . . Marie, is there anything else we can do for you?" Danny asked hopefully. "I mean, we're not in any hurry or anything."

"No, Danny, I don't need any more help. But thanks for offering." Marie shooed them out of the

97

kitchen. "Now run along, girls. I'll see you at campfire. I haven't felt much like participating the past few nights, but tonight I'm coming, and I'm going to sing at the top of my lungs!"

"I guess she doesn't know," Lynda murmured as they headed for the living room, "or she wouldn't be so nice."

"Marie's always nice," Emily said. "And so is Matt. That's why I feel so awful about what we did."

They paused outside the living-room door, and Caro said, "Well, I guess this is it. Good luck! We'll hang out at the camp store until it's over."

Libby squared her thin shoulders. "It's now or never, gang. Let's go!"

When the girls trudged into the living room, they found Matt standing in front of the big fieldstone fireplace, waiting for them. His lean, tanned face was solemn as they sat gingerly on the couch and the armchairs near the big television set with its VCR on which the campers often viewed tapes of movies and riding instruction. For a moment, nobody said anything. Then Matt said, "It seems there's been a series of misunderstandings lately, and I think it's time we set the record straight, don't you?"

Emily, Libby, Lynda, and Danny nodded in unison.

Matt shoved his hands in the pockets of his jeans. "Let's begin at the end for a change, rather than at the beginning. This afternoon I had a long talk with

98

Larry Frick, and he told me a lot of things I didn't know about before. But you did, didn't you?"

The girls nodded again.

Unexpectedly, Matt smiled. "Suppose you tell me your side of the story. I'm all ears."

Danny looked at Lynda, Lynda looked at Libby, Libby looked at Danny, and then they all looked at Emily. Emily looked at the floor. Then she raised her eyes to Matt's. "Well, it's this way . . ." she began, then cleared her throat because her voice came out in a little squeak and not like her regular voice at all. "It all began when Pam told us that Mr. Frick wanted to buy the camp," she continued in something that sounded more like her normal voice. "We were all very upset about that—"

"We were *devastated*," Danny said dramatically.

"It blew us away!" Libby added.

"So we decided—*I* decided—that we had to try to stop him," Emily went on. "The whole thing was my idea."

Lynda said, "But we all agreed—all of us. We couldn't stand the thought of Webster's being destroyed so Mr. Frick could put up vacation homes—"

"—and a shopping center," Danny said.

Matt raised his hands. "Please. One at a time! Emily started. Let her finish."

Emily took a deep breath. "Well, we decided that if Mr. Frick thought Webster's had problems—*big* problems—"

This time it was Matt who interrupted. "Like

99

being overrun with skunks, and having radioactive water because of a secret nuclear power plant, and an epidemic of Adirondack Blueberry Fever?"

"Yeah," Emily mumbled. "Like that."

Libby, who was incapable of sitting still for more than five minutes, scrambled out of her seat in a worn armchair and perched on one of its arms. "You gotta admit we were pretty creative!" she said with a shadow of her usual mischievous grin.

"Creative. Yes, I have to admit that, all right," Matt agreed. "Go on, Emily."

Emily shrugged. "Well, there's not much more to tell. We . . . well, we *lied* to Mr. Frick, that's all there is to it. But we didn't make him fall off his horse this afternoon! Honest, Matt, we had nothing to do with that!"

Matt nodded. "I know you didn't. If anyone's to blame for his accident, it's me. I should have warned him in time, but I didn't."

"He's all right, isn't he?" Danny asked anxiously. "Pam said he was, but he doesn't have any internal injuries or anything, does he?"

"Aside from a minor bruise on his posterior, Larry's in fine shape," Matt assured her. "But that's not the point, is it? The point is that you told him a lot of things that weren't true, and quite frankly, Larry feels that you've made a fool of him. And that hurts a lot more than any bruise."

Emily scrunched down into the sofa, wishing she could burrow under the cushions and just disap-

pear. "I know. What we did was wrong, and we're sorry."

"What you did was unkind," Matt said quietly. "I think you owe him an apology."

Lynda stood up. Looking Matt straight in the eye, she said, "We owe you an apology, too. We wanted to help you—and Marie and Pam and Warren and Chris—but we did just the opposite. Libby and I have been coming here for years. We should have known you wouldn't sell Webster's, no matter how much money you were offered. You love your horses as much as we do, maybe more. Like Emily said, we're really sorry."

Matt put an arm around her shoulders and walked with her to the sofa where Emily sat, huddled in misery. He sat down and put his other arm around Emily. Tears sprang to Emily's eyes, and she held herself away from him, biting her lower lip.

"Larry Frick isn't a bad guy, you know," Matt said gently. "He's okay when you get to know him. I wouldn't have considered making him a partner if I didn't like and trust him. Granted, he has a lot to learn about horses, but he's *willing* to learn. And he has an eight-year-old daughter who's as horse crazy as all of you are. She'd like to come to Webster's next summer as a Foal. But right now Larry's not too happy about that, or about becoming my partner, and you can hardly blame him, right?"

"Right," Emily mumbled.

"Webster's isn't going to go under if Larry decides he doesn't want to go in with me," Matt went on. "We may not be rich, but we're not suffering. So don't think that without Larry Frick, the camp won't survive. It will. But *with* Larry Frick, it'll be a bigger and better camp than it's ever been before. Are you willing to talk to him, back me up in what I've already told him—that all these stories you've told him are nothing more than very"—he glanced at Libby—"*creative* fabrications?"

"Oh, yes!" Emily cried, wiping the tears from her eyes with the back of her hand. "We'll tell him!" She leaned against Matt, and it was as though she were being held in her father's arms—warm and comfortable, and somehow like home.

"Then you're not going to punish us, or send us away from Webster's?" Danny quavered.

Matt laughed. "No, I don't think I'll do that! This year's crop of Fillies has made the summer decidedly interesting, to say the least."

"When would you like us to talk to Mr. Frick?" Emily asked.

"How about tomorrow afternoon?" Matt suggested. "I've persuaded him to meet me at the Winnepac Inn for lunch. We'll be back here around one o'clock." Suddenly he raised his voice. "Why don't the rest of you come in? It makes me nervous, knowing you're all listening at the door!"

Looking very sheepish, Caro, Penny, and Dru came into the room.

"We didn't think you'd hear us," Caro said. "And I know it's not polite to eavesdrop, but—well, we just had to know what was going on."

103

Matt smiled. "That's kind of what I figured." Then his smile faded, and he looked at each girl in turn. "I appreciate your trying to help, and I know your hearts are in the right place. But the next time you decide to be angels of mercy, check your facts, okay? And always tell the truth."

"I bet I know what Gram would say," Libby mused aloud. " 'Fools rush in where angels fear to tread.' Guess that's us, huh?"

Matt reached out and rumpled her red curls. "Your grandmother is a wise and wonderful woman!"

Chapter Nine

Promptly at one on Saturday afternoon, Emily and Libby showed up at the farmhouse as requested. They had decided to face Mr. Frick by themselves, and Danny and Lynda, after a few half-hearted protests, had agreed it might be better that way. Mr. Frick's shiny red car was parked by the mailbox, so they knew he and Matt had returned from their lunch in Winnepac.

"I hope their food was delicious," Libby said as they climbed the porch steps. "People are always in a better mood after a really good meal."

"More than anything, I hope Mr. Frick hasn't backed out of the deal with Matt," Emily said worriedly. "Does my hair look all right? Maybe we should have worn dresses or something. . . ."

Libby gave her a look. "You're beginning to sound like Caro! This isn't a tea party, remember. Mr. Frick isn't going to be less mad at us if we're all gussied up. Besides, I didn't even bring a dress to camp."

Emily sighed. "Neither did I. It was just a thought."

They walked slowly down the hall toward Matt's office where the fateful meeting was to be held and paused outside the closed door.

"I wish we didn't have to do this," Emily said in a small voice. "It wasn't so bad talking to Matt because he and the rest of the Websters are almost part of our family. But Mr. Frick definitely *isn't*."

"Look at it this way, Emily," Libby said. "This is our chance to make up for ruining things for Matt . . . or almost ruining them. The future of Webster's—the swimming pool, the tennis courts, new cabins, maybe even more horses—is in our hands!"

Emily couldn't help giggling, even nervous as she was. "If I sounded like Caro, *you* sounded like Danny just then."

"Yeah, Danny's pretty melodramatic sometimes. Maybe she'll be an actress when she grows up."

The girls looked at each other. "You know what we're doing, don't you?" Emily said. "We're stalling."

Libby nodded. "You're right. Let's do it." She rapped lightly on the door.

Matt opened it almost immediately. "Well, Libby and Emily." He smiled at them both, and they stared at him as though they had never seen him before. Instead of the riding clothes he usually wore, he was wearing a suit, a button-down shirt, and a striped tie. Seeing their surprised expressions, he said,

"Yes, I *do* own a suit, but only one. Come on in, girls. And while you and Mr. Frick are having a talk, I'm going upstairs to change."

Stricken, Emily said, "You mean you're not going to—"

"Help you out?" Matt finished for her. "Nope. You're on your own." Then he bent down and whispered in Emily's ear, "Don't worry. I promise that Mr. Frick doesn't bite!"

Libby and Emily walked into Matt's small office. They didn't pay any attention to all the photographs on the walls or the trophies and ribbons Matt had won that crowded the shelves. All they saw was Mr. Frick, who stood up from the leather chair in which he had been sitting.

"Have a seat, girls," he said and pointed to a worn, sagging couch opposite Matt's cluttered desk. He wasn't smiling.

They sat side by side, first removing a stack of horse magazines that had been piled on the couch. Mr. Frick leaned against Matt's desk, apparently waiting for either Emily or Libby to speak. Libby nudged Emily in the ribs, and Emily swallowed hard.

"Mr. Frick," she said, "I guess you know why we're here."

He nodded. "I think I do."

Emily glanced at Libby, who said all in a rush, "We're really sorry for all those things we told you about Webster's because they're not true and we only said them because we were afraid you were

107

going to buy Matt's property and tear everything down and mess everything up and that would be the end of the camp and the horses and everything and we didn't want that to happen because the Websters love this place and the horses, and we do, too!"

One corner of Mr. Frick's mouth twitched just a little. Was he going to smile? Emily wondered.

He didn't. He folded his arms across his chest and regarded the girls levelly. "I see," he said. "Matt told me something of the sort, but it took him a lot longer."

"Did you and Matt have a nice lunch?" Emily asked hopefully.

"Not bad." Mr. Frick wasn't about to be distracted. "What gave you the idea I was thinking of buying Webster's?"

So Emily told him what Pam had said, and why the Fillies had all jumped to conclusions. When she had finished, he said, "I see" again. There was a long, uncomfortable silence. Then, "Whose idea was the underground nuclear power plant near Schenectady?"

"Mine," Emily admitted. "It seemed like a good idea at the time. . . ."

"We weren't lying about the skunks, though," Libby added. "Foxy *did* run into a skunk, and that's why we were giving him a bath. But there aren't a whole lot of skunks around, no more than there are deer, and raccoons—"

"And birds, and squirrels," Emily added. "Webster's is just so *beautiful,* and we were afraid a lot of houses and stores would upset the ecology and turn it into something like . . . well, like Miami Beach!"

"You're right," Mr. Frick said. "That's one of the reasons I changed my mind about developing this area. It's peaceful and beautiful, and it ought to be preserved just as it is. That's why when Matt approached me about becoming his business partner, I jumped at the chance. Believe it or not, I love this place, too."

"You do?" Emily and Libby said together.

Mr. Frick went over to the leather armchair and sat back down. "Yes, I do. Does that surprise you?"

"Kind of," Libby confessed.

"Well, it shouldn't. I might not look like a nature lover, but appearances can be deceiving. I guess you're learning that, aren't you?"

"We sure are!" Emily said.

"So *are* you going to be Matt's partner?" Libby asked, leaning forward eagerly.

"We're awfully sorry we lied to you," Emily said. "We don't *usually* lie, and we never will again. You do believe us, don't you?"

Mr. Frick looked down at his folded hands. "Matt tells me you're both very good riders," he said at last, instead of answering Emily's question.

"Oh, Libby's a terrific rider," Emily said. "She's in the advanced class. I'm only an intermediate, but I've learned so much since I came here that I'm much better than I used to be."

Libby grinned. "I'm going to be a jockey, if I don't grow much bigger. And I probably won't because everyone in my family is short. My grandmother used to be a bareback rider in the circus, did you know that?"

Mr. Frick looked interested. "No, Matt didn't mention it." He turned to Emily. "And what about you? Are you going to be a jockey, too?"

Emily shook her head. "No way! I'm already too tall, even if I wanted to be, which I don't. What I really want to do is . . ." She felt herself blushing. "Do you really want to know?"

"Yes, I do."

"Well, I've decided that after my best friend, Judy, and I graduate from college, I want us to start a horse camp just like Webster's!"

"Is your friend Judy a camper, too?" Mr. Frick asked.

Emily explained about Judy's accident, and Mr. Frick nodded. "I see," he said a third time. There was another long silence. Emily and Libby glanced at each other, wondering what he was thinking.

Finally, Mr. Frick said, "Suppose we make a deal."

"A deal? What kind of a deal?" Libby asked.

"Sort of a business deal." Now Mr. Frick smiled. "No money involved, you understand. Call it a trade-off. You do what I ask, and I sign the papers making me Matt's partner. Sound good?"

"Uh . . ." Emily looked at Libby, and Libby frowned.

"We want to do anything that'll help Matt, but I think we ought to know what you have in mind before we agree," Libby said.

110

Mr. Frick's smile broadened. "Good for you! There's apparently a lot of business sense in that little red head. All right, here's what I have in mind. My daughter, Laura, is a horse nut. Don't ask me why, she just is."

"Matt told us she wants to be a Foal at Webster's next year," Emily said.

"Indeed she does. But in the meantime she's been driving her mother and me crazy, asking for riding lessons. I know there's only little more than a week left in the camp season, but I'd like the kid to have at least a taste of what she's going to encounter next summer at Webster's. The deal is this: The two of you start teaching Laura how to ride, and I'll become Matt's business partner."

Libby, who had been wriggling around on the sofa next to Emily, leaped to her feet. "Super! When do we start?"

"Well . . ." Mr. Frick got up, too, and went over to the door. He stuck his head out and hollered, "Laura? Laura, turn off the TV and come in here!"

A moment later, a bright-eyed, round-faced child in jeans and a T-shirt burst into the room, flinging her arms around Mr. Frick's waist. "Is it okay?" she cried, looking up at him. "Can I have lessons?"

Mr. Frick leaned down and gave her a hug. "You sure can, honeybunch. And these are your teachers—Emily Jordan and Libby Dexter."

Laura wriggled out of her father's embrace and trotted over to Emily and Libby. "Hi! Can we start right away? What kind of horse am I going to ride?

111

Maybe I better start with a pony—it isn't as far to the ground if I fall off, like Daddy did yesterday. Daddy's an *awful* rider! He has this humongous bruise on his—"

"*Laura!*" Mr. Frick yelled, turning bright red.

The little girl grinned. "Okay, Daddy, I won't tell where. Maybe you can teach him how to ride, too. But he doesn't love horses like I do. I collect model horses. . . . I have dozens of them! Can I meet my pony now? Gee, I can hardly wait!"

Mr. Frick looked at Emily and Libby. "Well, do you think you can handle this little bundle of energy?" He smiled at Laura, and Emily could tell that his daughter was the apple of his eye. Matt was right—Mr. Frick wasn't bad at all, once you got to know him.

"No problem," Libby said.

"Then we have a deal?" Mr. Frick stuck out his hand, and Emily shook it firmly.

"Deal!"

Chapter Ten

Half an hour later, Emily, Libby, and Laura were in the stable yard with Cupcake, a fat little Shetland pony. Emily had found an extra hard hat in the tack room, explaining one of the most important rules at Webster's to Laura: Never ride without a hat.

"Okay, Emily," Laura said cheerfully as Emily showed her how to fasten the chin strap. "It's awfully heavy, and it's hot, but I'll wear it if you say so."

"We say so," Libby told her. "It's so if you fall on your head, you don't crack your skull."

Laura giggled. "If I fall off, I'll probably land on my rear end, like Daddy did . . . oops!" She covered her mouth with her hand. "I promised I wouldn't tell!"

Emily grinned. "That's okay. We were there. We saw the whole thing."

"Did you laugh?" Laura asked.

"Oh, no. It's not funny when somebody falls off

a horse, because they might be badly hurt," Libby said.

"I'm glad you didn't laugh. Daddy just *hates* to be laughed at. Can I get on Cupcake now?"

Emily led the pony to the mounting block, and Libby said, "You always mount from the left side. Put your foot in the stirrup, and I'll give you a leg up."

"You don't have to. I can do it by myself." And Laura did, landing in the saddle with a solid thump. "Why do you have to mount from the left side? What will happen if you don't?"

"Gee, I don't know," Emily admitted. "That's just the way it is."

"I'll look it up when I get home," Laura said. "I have lots and lots of horse books. What do I do now?"

"You hold the reins like this." Emily showed her how. "Then you just sit there while we lead Cupcake to the riding ring."

"You don't have to lead him. Just don't go too far away in case I don't steer him right."

On the way to the ring, Laura kept up a steady stream of questions, which Emily and Libby answered as best they could. By the time they reached the ring, she had found out that they were both Fillies, how old they were, their horses' names, the names of their bunkmates, what their favorite colors were, and even what they'd had for lunch.

"I had lunch in the TV room at the farmhouse," Laura told them. "Mrs. Webster gave me a big, fat

114

tuna sandwich, and she let me watch *My Friend Flicka* on the VCR. I didn't see it all, though. Do you think I could see the rest after my lesson? Daddy said we were going to be here all afternoon because he and Mr. Webster had to sign some papers. He's going to be Mr. Webster's partner, did you know that?"

Emily and Libby glanced at each other. "We just found out," Emily said. "When did *you* find out?"

"Last night, when Daddy came home after he fell off his horse. He said everything was all settled, and I was so glad! If Daddy is Mr. Webster's partner, then I'm kind of part of Webster's, too, just like you, even though I'm not a camper yet."

"But—but he said—Matt said—" Libby sputtered.

"You know, Libby," Emily said thoughtfully, "I think Matt and Mr. Frick just did a number on us."

Libby nodded. "I think you're right. Laura's not the only one who's learning a lesson today!"

"What do you mean?" Laura asked. "What's a number? Like one, two, three? Are you having a lesson, too?"

"Here we are, Laura," Libby sang out. "Now the first thing you're going to do is walk Cupcake around the ring. Keep your elbows close to your sides and your hands steady."

"But you didn't answer me. What—"

"Yes, Laura, we're having a lesson, too," Emily said. "You know, your father is one smart business-man!"

Laura beamed with pride. "I know!"

115

Emily and the rest of the campers were grooming their mounts early the next afternoon in preparation for the weekly horse show when Emily heard a little voice that was now very familiar.

"Emily? Where are you? Libby, it's me, Laura! Guess what? Daddy and I are going to watch the show. Isn't that neat?"

Emily leaned out over Joker's stall door and waved. "I'm right here, Laura. Come say hello to my horse."

"Something tells me we're going to be seeing a lot of that little girl during the next week," Caro said as Laura trotted down the aisle between the stalls. Emily and Libby had told the other Fillies about their meeting with Mr. Frick, and about their new young pupil. And Laura, after her riding lesson was over and she had seen the rest of *My Friend Flicka*, had found her way to the Fillies' bunkhouse, where she had introduced herself and made herself at home. It had been all her father could do to pry her away and persuade her to go home for supper; if it had been up to Laura, she would have moved right in and spent the night.

"She's really a pretty cute kid," Emily said. "And I think she's going to be a good rider, too."

"Hi, Emily," Laura said, coming up beside her. "Is that Joker? He's beautiful! Can I help you brush him? Hi, Caro. That's Vic, right? Boy, is he *big*! I'd need a stepladder to get on him! Where's Libby? I want to meet Foxy. . . . Oh, there she is. Hi, Libby!

116

I'm coming to visit you, but first I want to see Cup-cake. I brought him a nice red apple. I don't want him to forget me."

She trotted off, and Caro said wryly, "I doubt if Cupcake will forget her—she won't give him a chance. I don't imagine *anybody* forgets Laura!"

"She's pretty memorable, all right," Emily agreed with a smile.

"Actually, she's sweet. I guess we can put up with her for one more week," Caro said.

"One more week . . ." Emily sighed, resting her cheek against Joker's glossy neck. "I just can't believe the summer's almost over. But at least we know Webster's will be here next year—and so will Joker."

"Are you going to write letters to him after you get back home?" Caro teased. "Maybe Chris would read them to him."

Emily pretended to be shocked. "Caro! What makes you think a horse as smart as Joker can't read?"

Laughing, Caro said, "Emily, you're crazy!"

"Yep, I am. Horse crazy!" Emily resumed brushing Joker, but she had hardly begun before Laura dashed up to the stall door.

Eyes shining below her thick brown bangs, she said, "Emily, guess what? Cupcake remembered me! I'm sure he did. And he ate the apple right up. I met Libby's horse, but he's not as pretty as Joker. I didn't tell him that, though. Hey, Emily, do you think maybe I could ride Cupcake for a few minutes before the horse show starts? It doesn't begin until two, and it's only"—she looked at her Mickey Mouse watch—"ten minutes after one. Could I, Emily? Please? Because I kind of told Daddy he could see me ride, and he wants to, so can I? I asked Libby and she said she'd saddle him for me— Cupcake, I mean, not Daddy!"

Emily shrugged helplessly and laughed. "Do I have a choice?"

A little while later, Laura, wearing the same riding hat as yesterday, was scrambling aboard the pony in the stable yard. Emily reminded her how to hold the reins, but Laura hadn't forgotten. She dug her heels into Cupcake's plump sides, and Emily walked along beside her until they reached the advanced riding ring.

"This is where I told Daddy I'd be," Laura said. "Can we go in?"

"Afraid not," Emily said. "Warren and Chris are setting up the jumps. They wouldn't like us getting in their way."

Laura peered into the ring. "Will you and Libby teach me to jump? Can Cupcake jump, or is he too fat?"

"I don't think you're going to be ready for jumping for a while yet," Emily told her firmly. "And neither will Cupcake."

Laura looked crestfallen for a moment, then brightened. "Well, okay. But I bet I'd learn real quick. You remember in *Gone With the Wind* when Bonnie Blue Butler tries to jump her pony, only the jump is too high and she falls off and breaks her neck? I *hate* that part! But I bet the only reason she fell off was because she was wearing that long dress and riding sidesaddle. Now I'd never do a dumb thing like that! I'm going to be the best rider in the world one of these days."

"I wouldn't be surprised," Emily said. "But in the meantime, let's just walk Cupcake around the outside of the ring until your father gets here."

"Okay," Laura said cheerfully. "Giddyap, Cupcake! Do you think he knows what 'giddyap' means? It's a funny word, isn't it? I wonder why you say 'giddyap' to a horse when you want him to go, and 'whoa' when you want him to stop. . . . Oh, hi, Daddy! Look at me! I'm riding all by myself!"

"So I see." Mr. Frick came over to the pony and patted him on the head—as if Cupcake were a dog, Emily thought, suppressing a smile. Mr. Frick looked much more relaxed today in slacks and a short-sleeved polo shirt. He also looked very happy, and very proud of his little girl. "Afternoon, Emily. All ready for the show?"

"Yes, sir. Is Mrs. Frick coming to see it?"

"No, she's out of town this weekend. Laura and I are on our own till tomorrow."

"Daddy, watch me! I'm going to ride over to that tree and back," Laura said, and she and Cupcake trundled off.

"Uh . . . Mr. Frick, are you and Matt partners now?" Emily asked shyly.

"After a trip to the lawyer's office on Wednesday

we will be." Mr. Frick smiled at her. "We made a deal, remember? You and Libby have kept your part of the bargain, and I'll keep mine."

"But you were going to do it anyway, weren't you? Even before we made our deal." The words popped out before Emily could stop them.

Mr. Frick raised his brows. "Now whatever gave you that idea?" He glanced over at Laura. "Oh, I see. Guess I should have figured that that little imp would spill the beans," he said, grinning. "You're right. I didn't think it would do any harm to keep you in suspense a little longer, considering how you girls tried to fool me. But no harm done, right? Everything's worked out just fine."

"Yes, it has, thank goodness!" Emily agreed. She decided she was beginning to like Mr. Frick very much.

"Did you watch me every minute, Daddy?" Laura asked excitedly, bringing Cupcake to a halt beside her father. "Didn't I do good? Emily and Libby are good teachers, aren't they? Why don't you let them teach you to ride? I bet you'd learn real fast."

"We'll see about that, honeybunch," Mr. Frick said. "But for the moment, I think they'll have their hands full with you. You're not being a pest, are you, Laura? Not talking their ears off, or bothering them with too many questions?"

"Who, me?" Laura's round face was the picture of innocence. "Oh, no! I'm as quiet as a mouse, aren't I, Emily?"

Emily cocked her head to one side, considering.

121

"Well, maybe a *noisy* mouse," she said at last. Then she grinned. "You know something? I just had a great idea!"

Mr. Frick looked apprehensive. "Seems to me your last 'great idea' kind of backfired, didn't it?"

"Yes, but this one won't," Emily assured him. "Laura, how would you like to be the Fillies' mascot from now on? Since you're going to be around a lot, we'll show you the ropes so when you're a Foal next summer, you'll know exactly what to expect."

Laura was so excited that she bounced up and down in the saddle. "Oh, boy! The Fillies' mascot! Wait till I tell Mom! Isn't that super, Daddy? What does a mascot do? Can I sleep over some night in the empty bunk over Caro's? Will you teach me to saddle Cupcake all by myself? Can I meet some of the Foals? Do you think they'll like me? It's all right with you, isn't it, Daddy? Please say yes!"

As Mr. Frick wholeheartedly agreed, Emily couldn't help wondering what she'd gotten herself into. The last week of camp promised to be very interesting indeed!

Camp is almost over—except for the final competition and Parents' Night. And the Websters have one last surprise in store for the girls: They're going to make a video of the campers in action with their horses. Only Emily and her friends fancy themselves movie stars and can't resist a few ad-libbed performances of their own! But will a video of Webster's Country Horse Camp and her favorite horse, Joker, be enough to keep Emily happy until next summer?

Don't miss HORSE CRAZY #6
Riding Home by Virginia Vail

ABOUT THE AUTHOR

Virginia Vail is a pseudonym of the author of over a dozen young adult novels, most recently the ANIMAL INN series. She is the mother of two grown children, both of whom are animal lovers, and lives in Forest Hills, New York with one fat gray cat. Many years ago, Virginia Vail fell in love with a beautiful palomino named Joker. She always wanted to put him in a book. Now she has.